Holy Week

Ohio University Press Polish and Polish-American Studies Series

Series Editor: John J. Bukowczyk

Framing the Polish Home: Postwar Cultural Constructions of Hearth, Nation, and Self, edited by Bożena Shallcross

Traitors and True Poles: Narrating a Polish-American Identity, 1880–1939, by Karen Majewski

Auschwitz, Poland, and the Politics of Commemoration, 1945–1979, by Jonathan Huener

The Exile Mission: The Polish Political Diaspora and Polish-Americans, 1939–1956, by Anna D. Jaroszyńska-Kirchmann

The Grasinski Girls: The Choices They Had and the Choices They Made, by Mary Patrice Erdmans

Testaments: Two Novellas of Emigration and Exile, by Danuta Mostwin

The Clash of Moral Nations: Cultural Politics in Piłsudski's Poland, 1926–1935, by Eva Plach

Holy Week: A Novel of the Warsaw Ghetto Uprising, by Jerzy Andrzejewski

Holy Week

A Novel of the
Warsaw Ghetto Uprising

Jerzy Andrzejewski

Introduction and Commentary
by Oscar E. Swan

Foreword by Jan Gross

OHIO UNIVERSITY PRESS

ATHENS

Ohio University Press, Athens, Ohio 45701
www.ohio.edu/oupress
© 2007 by Ohio University Press

Printed in the United States of America
All rights reserved

Ohio University Press books are printed on acid-free paper ♾

14 12 11 10 09 08 07 06   5 4 3 2 1
Cover image: Still from the motion picture *Wielki Tydzień* (*Holy Week*). Courtesy of
Andrzej Wajda

Library of Congress Cataloging-in-Publication Data

Andrzejewski, Jerzy, 1909–1983.
  [Wielki Tydzień. English]
  Holy Week : a novel of the Warsaw Ghetto Uprising / Jerzy Andrzejewski ;
introduction and commentary by Oscar E. Swan ; foreword by Jan Gross.
       p. cm. — (Ohio University Press Polish and Polish-American studies series)
  Includes bibliographical references.
  ISBN-13: 978-0-8214-1715-7 (cloth : alk. paper)
  ISBN-10: 0-8214-1715-0 (cloth : alk. paper)
  ISBN-13: 978-0-8214-1716-4 (pbk. : alk. paper)
  ISBN-10: 0-8214-1716-9 (pbk. : alk. paper)
  1. Warsaw (Poland)—History—Warsaw Ghetto Uprising, 1943—Fiction. I. Swan, Oscar
E. II. Title.
  PG7158.A7W5413 2007
  891.8'537—dc22

                                                            2006024584

Publication of books in the Polish and Polish-American Studies Series has been made possible in part by the generous support of the following organizations:

> Polish American Historical Association, New Britain, Connecticut

> Stanislaus A. Blejwas Endowed Chair in Polish and Polish American Studies, Central Connecticut State University, New Britain, Connecticut

> The Polish Institute of Arts and Sciences of America, Inc., New York, New York

> The Piast Institute: An Institute for Polish and Polish American Affairs, Detroit, Michigan

> Additional support for this book has been provided by the Richard D. and Mary Jane Edwards Endowed Publication Fund, University of Pittsburgh

Contents

Foreword

AS A BRILLIANT NOVELIST and prose writer, Jerzy Andrzejewski is a rare specimen in the firmament of Polish literature, which abounds in extraordinarily talented poets. Two of his contemporaries, Czesław Miłosz and Wisława Szymborska, received the Nobel Prize for Literature in 1980 and 1996 respectively, and while Andrzejewski lived, there was an aura of expectation that he would be awarded a Nobel as well.

Andrzejewski's literary career spanned the entire short twentieth century and a gamut of ideological positions. Just before the war in 1939, he received the much-coveted Young Authors' Prize of the Polish Academy of Literature for a collection of short stories and his novel *Mode of the Heart* (*Ład serca*), and he was hailed as a rising star of Catholic literature. Shortly after the war, his novel *Ashes and Diamonds* (*Popiół i diament*) was widely admired as an artistically brilliant portrayal of the new political era that had dawned in Poland with the accession to power of the Communist Party. Later this book was turned into a cult film by director Andrzej Wajda and gained international acclaim. Andrzejewski was lionized by the new regime, and his intellectual fascination with the new aesthetics of Socialist Realism was dissected in major works of literary criticism, including, among others, *The Captive Mind,* which his friend Miłosz wrote after going into exile in the West.

Holy Week gives artistic representation to what became for a number of distinguished Polish intellectuals a dramatic realization—the abandonment of the Jews to Nazi persecution by the dominant Polish society. Naturally, the story line of *Holy Week* and its moral and existential dilemmas are all-important for the development of the individual characters. But of crucial importance in the narrative is the background of the Warsaw Ghetto uprising. A number of great Polish writers (notably Adolf Rudnicki and Mieczysław Jastrun, both of whom were assimilated Jews) have noted the callous indifference of Warsaw's inhabitants to the tragic fate of the insurgents and the remaining residents of the ghetto. A steady shower of ashes sifted down for days from a cloudless sky as German SS and police detachments charged with suppressing the uprising set fire to this part of the city, and to its Jewish population, creating the greatest conflagration in Warsaw's history.

In addition to Andrzejewski's novel, which offered the first artistic examination of the drama, the events of the ghetto uprising inspired works by other writers. Miłosz wrote a stunning poem on the subject published after the war in his volume *The Rescue* (*Ocalenie*). Miłosz and Andrzejewski were the closest of friends during the Second World War, which they endured together in Warsaw. They worked together—quite literally, for it was a handmade edition of only a few dozen copies—on the underground publication of Miłosz's *Poems* (*Wiersze*), written under the pseudonym Jan Syruć. The imagination and sensitivity of the two friends were tuned in the same key. They saw each other every day, and when Andrzejewski moved with his family to a larger apartment across town from the Miłoszes, they wrote long letters to each other, which Miłosz published much later in a volume of correspondence, *Legends of Modernity* (*Legendy nowoczesności*).

After 1956, following the period of "thaw" and de-Stalinization in the Soviet bloc countries, Andrzejewski became one of the most outspoken members of the critical intelligentsia. In time he turned in his party card, signed petitions demanding greater freedom of expression in artistic and political fields, and was recognized as an iconic figure of intellectual opposition to the Communist regime in Poland. When Poland joined with other Soviet bloc countries in the 1968 invasion of Czechoslovakia—to suppress Alexander Dubček's "socialism with a human face" and the liberalization of the Czechoslovak regime—Andrzejewski wrote a public letter of apology and solidarity addressed to Eduard Goldstücker, president of the Czechoslovak Union of Writers, which had been at the forefront of the movement for reform. In 1976, he was among the founders of the Workers' Defense Committee (Komitet Obrony Robotników, KOR) in Poland, an unprecedented initiative in which intellectuals openly provided legal and financial assistance to workers repressed by the Communist regime after a wave of strikes. KOR transformed politics in the Soviet bloc and led directly to the formation of the Solidarity movement in August 1980.

Jerzy Andrzejewski's creative powers slowly waned, succumbing to alcoholism. In spite of his progressively incapacitating illness, he left a formidable oeuvre that is compelling not only because of his skills as a storyteller but because, like all great literature of the twentieth century, it bears testimony to the fragility of the human condition.

Jan T. Gross
Princeton University

Series Editor's Preface

Jerzy Andrzejewski may be best known in the West as the author of the screenplay for *Ashes and Diamonds*, the great postwar film by Polish director Andrzej Wajda. Andrzejewski, though, was a monumental figure in post–World War II Polish literature with both a broad canon of work in literature and a heroic record of participation in Poland's anti-Communist Solidarity movement.

Among Andrzejewski's many achievements was a little book, ironically titled *Holy Week*, which arguably ranks among his most interesting and significant works. Although virtually unknown among English-language readers, *Holy Week* merits attention as one of the first attempts by Polish intellectuals during the postwar period to confront the problem of anti-Semitism in Polish society.

Holy Week, which we publish here for the first time in English translation, is a troubling story of failed human possibilities set against the backdrop of the destruction of the Warsaw Ghetto by the Nazis. It is a story of love and fear, of ethnic bigotry and Christian charity, of heroism and victimhood, of human weakness and societal limits. As such, it draws out moral lessons—for persons and peoples—about the toll that prejudice takes on individuals' humanity and on national self-identity. In its own imperfect way, it marked the beginning of a great national moral self-examination in Poland, one that has proceeded only in fits and starts since the end of the war but has gained momentum since the end of Poland's Communist regime and, in large measure, has revolutionized Polish national values and sensibilities regarding the country's Jewish minority.

In bringing out this edition of *Holy Week* at this time, we hope to encourage a continuation of the dialogue and introspection inspired by the papal visits to the former Nazi German concentration camp Auschwitz-Birkenau, the recent publication of such works as Jan Gross's *Neighbors*, and the revival of Jewish culture in contemporary Poland, as well as by other political events and developments in Polish society that suggest some resurgence in right-wing Polish nationalism. We no less believe that the publication of this work also should serve to honor and memorialize its author and other Poles possessed of the courage and integrity to plumb this dark recess within the otherwise noble heart of their country. May it also warn just and righteous men and women of all nations, creeds, and races against intolerance in thought, words, and deeds now and in the future.

Publication of the Ohio University Press Polish and Polish-American Studies Series marks a milestone in the maturation of the Polish studies field and stands as a fitting tribute to the scholars and organizations whose efforts have brought it to fruition. Supported by a series advisory board of accomplished Polonists and Polish-Americanists, the Polish and Polish-American Studies Series has been made possible through generous financial assistance from the Polish American Historical Association, the Polish Institute of Arts and Sciences of America, the Stanislaus A. Blejwas Endowed Chair in Polish and Polish American Studies at Central Connecticut State University, and the Piast Institute and through institutional support from Wayne State University and Ohio University Press. Publication of this particular series volume has been aided by a grant from the Richard D. and Mary Jane Edwards Endowed Publication Fund at the University of Pittsburgh, the home institution of the volume's principal translator, Professor Oscar Swan, whose efforts to bring this project to fruition also should be especially recognized here. The series meanwhile has benefited from the warm encouragement of a number of other persons, including Gillian Berchowitz, M. B. B. Biskupski, the late Stanislaus A. Blejwas, Mary Erdmans, Thaddeus Gromada, James S. Pula, Thaddeus Radzilowski, and David Sanders. The moral and material support from all of these institutions and individuals is gratefully acknowledged.

John J. Bukowczyk

Acknowledgments and Notes
on the Translation

THIS TRANSLATION OF Jerzy Andrzejewski's *Holy Week* began as a group project in an advanced Polish language course at the University of Pittsburgh. Class members Daniel M. Pennell, Anna M. Poukish, and Matthew J. Russin contributed to the translation; the instructor, Oscar E. Swan, was responsible for the overall accuracy and stylistic unity of the translation as well as for the biographical and critical notes and essays.

Polish first names are preserved in the form in which they appear in the text (whether *Anna* or *Ania, Józef, Józek,* or *Józio,* for example). The last names of female characters, normally ending in *-ska, -cka,* are given as *-ski, -cki* when preceded by titles, otherwise as *-ska, -cka;* hence *Mrs. Piotrowski,* but *Piotrowska,* both referring to the same person. For the most part, place names have not been anglicized, except for Warsaw, the Vistula River, and occasional other instances where straightforward English translations suggest themselves, for example, Savior Square for Plac Zbawiciela, or Saxon Garden for Ogród Saski. The translators identified a number of instances where they felt commentary was needed for greater clarity, and it is given in ordered notes, gathered at the end of the volume.

Thanks are due to Andrzej Wajda for permitting the illustration of this work with stills from his 1996 film *Wielki Tydzień.* Julie Draskoczy and Helena Goscilo at the University of Pittsburgh commented helpfully on the translation, as did the editors at Ohio University Press. Ricky S. Huard, project editor at Ohio University Press, deserves credit as a virtual second translator. Facts concerning Jerzy Andrzejewski's life are based primarily on *Andrzejewski* by Anna Synoradzka (Warsaw: Wydawnictwo Literackie, 1997). The photograph of Andrzejewski was provided by the Muzeum Literatury in Warsaw.

Jerzy Andrzejewski. Photo courtesy of Muzeum Literatury, Warsaw

Note on the Author

JERZY ANDRZEJEWSKI (1909–83), one of modern Poland's most versatile prose writers and one of the best known outside Poland, was born in Warsaw. He attended the University of Warsaw from 1927 to 1931, where he majored in Polish literature but left without receiving a degree. His first collection of short stories, *Unavoidable Roads* (*Drogi nieuknknione*), appeared in 1936, followed by the widely acclaimed novel *Mode of the Heart* (*Ład serca*). During the Second World War, he was active in the literary underground. His first postwar novels were *Holy Week,* published as part of the volume *Night* (*Noc,* 1945), and the much better known *Ashes and Diamonds* (*Popiół i diament,* 1948), which dealt with the adjustments Poles had to make following their country's forced entry into the Soviet sphere of influence. These works established Andrzejewski's reputation as a writer of moral conflict and dilemma in the tradition of the French existentialists.

Before the war, Andrzejewski had been an outspoken opponent of the intrusion of politics into literature. In the early postwar years, however, he increasingly accommodated himself to the political reality of the time, joining the Polish United Workers' Party (Polska Zjednoczona Partia Robotnicza) in 1950. He soon thereafter published an infamous manifesto in which he subjected his previous work to criticism and pledged allegiance to Marxist doctrine. Throughout the early 1950s, he played the role of publicist and ardent spokesman for the party line.

The year 1954 found Andrzejewski politically sanitizing a new edition of *Ashes and Diamonds,* which became required reading in the schools. In the same year, however, he published a collection of short stories whose title piece, *The Gold Fox* (*Złoty lis*), is a thinly veiled critique of the oppressive effect of socialist reality on imagination, creativity, and interpersonal and family relations. This work became one of the literary landmarks of Poland's literary and political "thaw" following the death of Stalin and preceded by a number of years the appearance of similar literature in the Soviet Union.

From that point on, Andrzejewski directed his literary and journalistic activities toward the goal of carving out for himself the role of spokesman for progressive currents in Polish cultural life. *Darkness Covers the Earth* xvi | *Note on the Author*

(*Ciemności kryją ziemię,* 1957), a historical novel set in the time of the Span-
ish Inquisition, can be read without much imagination as a condemnation of
the Stalinist mentality, the Communist political machine, and the doctrine
of the ends justifying the means. For his efforts, Andrzejewski found himself and his works under increasingly harsh scrutiny and censorship, especially under the Gomułka regime through the late 1950s and 1960s.

In 1963 Andrzejewski was among the 34 signatories of a famous letter of
protest to the Communist authorities over the stifling conditions then pre-
vailing in Polish cultural life. In 1975 he was among the most active of the 101
signatories of a letter to the Constitutional Commission, protesting changes
in the Polish constitution in favor of the Soviet Union. Andrzejewski was also
among the first 14 members of the Workers' Defense Committee (Komitet
Obrony Robotników, KOR), which arose in response to the repression of
worker strikes in 1976, a cornerstone of the Polish freedom movement that
eventually culminated in the rise of the Solidarity trade union and the fall of
Communism in Poland following the elections of 1989, an event the author did
not live to see.

Between 1960 and 1980 Andrzejewski published a stream of new novels,
a body of work remarkable for its stylistic and thematic variety, which se-
cured for him a position as of one of Poland's most significant twentieth-
century novelists. Of greatest importance are *The Gates of Paradise* (*Bramy
raju,* 1960), *He Cometh Leaping upon the Mountains* (*Idzie skacząc po
górach,* 1963), *The Appeal* (*Apelacja,* 1967), *Mishmash* (*Miazga,* 1981), and *Nobody* (*Nikt,* 1982).

The author died of a heart attack in Warsaw in 1983 and is buried in
Powązki cemetery.

Note on the Warsaw Ghetto Uprising

THE WARSAW GHETTO UPRISING was the largest and symbolically most important Jewish uprising during World War II and the first urban uprising in German-occupied Europe.

In the summer of 1942, around three hundred thousand Jews were deported from the Warsaw Ghetto to Treblinka. When reports of the mass murder of the deportees leaked back, a group of survivors formed the Jewish Fighting Organization (Żydowska Organizacja Bojowa) under the command of Mordecai Anielewicz. Right-wing Zionists formed another resistance organization, the Jewish Fighting Union (Żydowski Związek Wojskowy). The two groups decided to cooperate to oppose German attempts to destroy the ghetto.

In January 1943, using a small supply of smuggled weapons, members of the Jewish resistance infiltrated a column of deportees and began firing upon the German troops. Although the Germans succeeded in deporting some five thousand to sixty-five hundred people, after a few days the troops retreated. This momentary victory inspired the ghetto fighters to prepare for future resistance, among other things by building a network of underground bunkers.

On April 19, 1943, German troops and police entered the ghetto to deport its remaining inhabitants, and the Warsaw Ghetto uprising began. Some 750 fighters, using mostly small arms and grenades smuggled into the ghetto by the Polish resistance, fought the heavily armed and well-trained German army.

On the third day of the uprising, in order to force the remaining Jews out of hiding, troops under the command of SS General Jürgen Stroop began to systematically burn the ghetto, building by building. Anielewicz and those with him were killed in an attack on his command bunker, which fell to German forces on May 8. By May 16, 1943, after nearly a month of resistance, the ghetto was in ruins and the revolt had ended. General Stroop ordered the Great Synagogue on Tłomacki Street destroyed as a symbol of German victory. Stroop reported that he had captured 56,065 Jews and destroyed 631 bunkers. He estimated that his units had killed as many as seven thousand

Jews. Another seven thousand were deported to Treblinka to be killed. The remainder of the ghetto inhabitants were deported to the Poniatowa, Trawniki, and Majdanek concentration camps.

The last commander of the Jewish uprising, Marek Edelman, survived the war and became a prominent physician in Łódź. As of this writing, he is still alive and politically active.

INTRODUCTION ⫴
Jerzy Andrzejewski's *Holy Week*

JERZY ANDRZEJEWSKI'S NOVEL *Holy Week* deserves recognition as one of the most significant literary works to appear in Poland in the years immediately after the war. Its absorbing and tightly knit plot, its nearly documentary realism, and the momentous nature of the subject matter—the Warsaw Ghetto uprising of 1943—set it apart from its contemporaries. Few fictional works dealing with the Second World War have been written so close in time to the events themselves. None treats as honestly the range of Polish attitudes toward the Jews at the height of the Nazi extermination campaign.

Andrzejewski's novel, or novella, has been infrequently reprinted. It has not been widely translated into languages other than German (editions in 1948, 1950, 1964, and 1966). The relative popularity of the work in Germany probably stems from the fact that it is a story about the Holocaust in which Poles, not Germans, are the primary actors. The 1993 Polish edition, on which the present translation is based, lists the dates of the novel as 1943–45; the two years refer to two different versions of the same story. The earlier and shorter version was never published, and its manuscript has not surfaced. It is known only from the recollections of listeners to whom it was read in secret wartime literary gatherings. Apparently it focused on the moral dilemma of the protagonist, Jan Malecki, a recently married Pole upon whom is thrust the decision whether to shelter a Jewish woman acquaintance.

Andrzejewski had always been an outspoken critic of anti-Semitism. One possible factor prompting him to rewrite the first version of *Holy Week*, giving greater prominence to the largely apathetic attitude of the Poles toward the Jewish uprising, was the appearance in the immediate postwar period of anti-Jewish manifestations across the south of Poland, particularly in Rzeszów, Tarnów, and Kraków. The statement of the fascist Zalewski, that one can be grateful to Hitler for having resolved the "Jewish question," mirrors declarations made at various postwar right-wing political gatherings.

In *Holy Week*, as in many of Andrzejewski's works, personal considerations begin to overshadow abstract questions of right and wrong and to affect the decision-making ability of the main character. Jan Malecki feels increasingly estranged from the irritating Jewish woman, Irena Lilien, with whom he had once been close, and wonders whether he has done the right thing by risking the safety of his family (his wife, Anna, is pregnant) to save her. Irena, for her part, has been inalterably changed by the traumas of her wartime experiences. A member of a prominent, privileged, and acculturated Jewish family of banking and academe before the war, she has been forced for the first time in her life to think of herself as a Jew, because that is how others now view her. Importantly for the plot, Irena has a distinctively Semitic appearance.

The rewritten version of the novel adds to the personal dilemma of the central character the broader context of Poles' attitudes toward the "Jewish question" and the plight of the Jews locked in the ghetto during the final moments of its existence in 1943. In both its versions, *Holy Week* by all accounts went over among listeners and readers like a lead balloon. Critics passed over the work largely in silence. Andrzej Wajda's film version of the novel, issued some fifty years later in 1995, had a similar reception. Andrzejewski's work touched—and still touches—a number of raw nerves, which one would do well to enumerate here.

Poles, having lost a greater percentage of their people than any other nation in a Holocaust in which percentages and numbers ceased to have meaning, were in no mood in 1945 to read about a temporizing hero's vacillations over whether to harbor a Jew during the war. Even less interested were they in reading about Polish anti-Semitism, the whole gamut of which is openly and honestly displayed on the pages of this novel, seemingly for the first time in all of Polish literature. For their part, Jewish readers were loath to appreciate a novel on the ghetto uprising as seen from the outside, whose protagonists were Poles and in which the central Jewish character is a spoiled, whiny, and self-centered young woman.

Some readers questioned the decency of fictionalizing events so horrific as to defy any recounting other than the documentary and statistical. The ease with which Andrzejewski moved from real-life human drama to fictional depiction before the ashes had even cooled, as it were, scandalized some for whom the war was not the setting for an action novel, but their own personal experience as well as that of numerous friends, relatives, and comrades who had not survived. Of course, equally justifiable reservations regarding facile fictionalization could be raised regarding the author's much more positively received work, *Ashes and Diamonds* (*Popiół i diament,* 1949)—and they were raised, but without impugning that novel's status as one of the major literary monuments of postwar Central European literature.

It is true that Andrzejewski applies the niceties of the prewar novel of moral choice to a wartime situation unprecedented in its terror, brutality, atrocities, and sheer level of destruction—a feature some readers found disconcerting. One of the novel's main themes, however, is the very inadequacy of the attitudes, values, and traditions with which the prewar Polish intelligentsia had been imbued. Indeed, they had negative survival value in dealing with a historical cataclysm of such magnitude that it indifferently and indiscriminately crushed everything and everyone before it, whatever their attitudes or actions.

There was also the question of the author's political motives. The Soviets were now in power, and Andrzejewski was perceived by some as currying favor with the authorities by casting prewar Polish bourgeois society as by and large indifferent to the plight of a sizable and ethnically distinct segment of its population.

It is not endearing to the public in Poland for an author to criticize either the Catholic Church or the Polish national character. Although Andrzejewski does not exactly do either, the pages of *Holy Week* are nevertheless saturated with the irony of a situation in which workaday Warsaw citizens, under the canopy of an immense cloud of smoke, baked Easter loaves, bought flowers, rode merry-go-rounds, mouthed pieties, and crowded the churches against a background of constant gunfire and street executions of Jewish escapees. The novel virtually forces the Polish reader to recognize himself among the busy shoppers and idle onlookers at the spectacle of the ghetto's last days. The novel's very title and the device of using the days of Holy Week to chronicle the stage-by-stage demise of the ghetto uprising underscore the irony that reaches its peak on Good Friday, the day in the New Testament calendar on which the Jews demanded Christ's crucifixion.

The immediacy with which *Holy Week* strikes the reader stems in no little part from the author's presence as an eyewitness to the actual historical events. Together with Maria Abgarowicz, his future wife, the author occupied an apartment on Nowiniarska Street that looked out not only on the walls of the ghetto but also on the carousel being set up for the Easter holidays. This carousel, on which merrymakers rode, brushing ashes out of their hair while the ghetto burned its last, was the one immortalized by Czesław

The church at Wawrzyszew. Photo by O. Swan

Miłosz in his poem "Campo di Fiori." The apartment house became the model for the setting of Jan Malecki's surprise encounter with Irena Lilien on the first day of the Jewish uprising.

Andrzejewski later moved with Maria, who was by that time pregnant with their son Marcin, to a house in the northern Warsaw suburb of Bielany, the site of the fictional villa populated by Jan, his pregnant wife, and a cross-section of other Warsaw inhabitants ranging from the seedy and bigoted Piotrowski family to the landlord Zamojski, with his aristocratic last name, elegant library, and liveried servant. Warsaw streetcar number 17, which Jan rides to and from town, still wends its way from Mokotów in the south, through downtown, and along the ghost walls of the ghetto, to arrive finally in Bielany, now more firmly incorporated into the city limits than it was in 1943. To the west of Bielany still lies the settlement of Wawrzyszew, with its connected ponds and small church near which Anna prays.

The fictional name Irena Lilien may have been taken from a family with whom the author briefly stayed in Lwów following his flight from Warsaw in 1939. Andrzejewski himself stated that her character was modeled on Janina Askenazy, the daughter of the renowned historian Szymon Askenazy. Most others have identified the prototype as Wanda Wertenstein, Andrzejewski's companion from 1941 to 1943, a prominent Polish postwar film critic. Irena's picture is undoubtedly a composite.

Andrzejewski has been characterized by Czesław Miłosz as a dramatist in a novelist's garb. Indeed, the novel's action takes place within a compressed period of time, Tuesday through Friday of Holy Week, and largely within the confines of the Maleckis' Bielany apartment, from which forays into the city provide an ever-changing dramatic contrast. The action is propelled almost entirely by the direct speech of the characters, whose every utterance is accompanied by such specific descriptions of voice, tone, gesture, and attitude as to make the transformation of the novel into a play or film seem anticipated. Wajda's film transcribes entire passages from the novel nearly verbatim.

The characters also seem chosen according to the principle of dramatic economy: each represents a type, and no type is represented by more than one character. The three main characters (leaving aside Irena for the moment)—the architect Malecki, his wife Anna, and his younger brother Julek—seem typecast according to the canons of Polish literature stretching back to the nineteenth century. Irena herself, whose options for action are limited by external circumstances, and who therefore plays a passive and reactive role, is not so much a literary stereotype as she is a lost individual, hounded and doomed by an unjust fate.

Malecki is the ratiocinating and rationalizing liberal. He has all the right instincts and sensibilities but is unable to act on them in a direct and timely fashion. In his occasional moments of clarity he realizes that his every move has been taken in service of his own ease and comfort. Anna is the veritable embodiment of the *Matka Polka* (Polish Mother)—warm, nurturing, instinctively moral, deeply religious, and committed to family and fatherland (*ojczyzna*). Julek is Malecki's polar opposite in all ways, including his rejection of hearth and home for the national cause. Although the character has been criticized for being left-leaning, nothing Julek says allows one to pin a specific political affiliation on him. His values lie outside himself, and he is committed to giving them embodiment through action.

Andrzejewski would have been among the last to downplay Poland's heroic resistance to the German occupation or the suffering endured by the Polish population at large; in fact, this suffering is a major motif in the novel.

Anna Malecka loses almost her entire family in the war, whether in the initial invasion, in prison camps, or through random misfortune. One may add to this the barely alluded-to tragedies of the Makarczyński and Makowski families and the unnamed next-door neighbors taken away in the middle of the night. Thousands of instances have been documented in which Poles risked their own lives and those of others to save and shelter Jews, more than in any other country. Authorial honesty, however, demanded that not every moment of a novel about the ghetto uprising be draped in the national flag. Not every Pole played the role of hero; among them were extortionists, informers, collaborators, and outright fascists and Nazi sympathizers. The Polish underground resistance group Żegota, while sympathetic to the Jewish cause, judged that the time was not yet ripe for a general open revolt against the Nazis and provided only token help to the insurgents: handguns and a few rifles and hand grenades. Most Poles, even if they were troubled about the plight of the Jews, went through the war as did Jan Malecki—carefully, one step at a time, doing their everyday jobs and looking after their own interests. Often they were successful in tiptoeing around disaster, though sometimes they were not.

Much of Polish literature is inaccessible to a broader audience, not only because of the language barrier but also because of the specific national problems occupying the minds of many Polish writers. Such criticism cannot be raised with respect to *Holy Week*, which is, perhaps, more easily appreciated by an English-speaking readership than by the postwar Polish audience for whom the novel was originally intended.

Guide to Pronunciation

THE FOLLOWING KEY provides a guide to the pronunciation of Polish words and names.

a is pronounced as in *father*

c as ts in *cats*

ch like a guttural h, as in German *Bach*

cz as hard ch in *church*

g (always hard) as in *get*

i as ee, as in *meet*

j as y, as in *yellow*

rz as hard zh, as in French *jardin*

sz as hard sh, as in *ship*

szcz as hard shch, as in *fresh cheese*

u as oo, as in *boot*

w as v, as in *vat*

ć as soft ch, as in *cheap*

ś as soft sh, as in *sheep*

ż as hard zh, as in French *jardin*

ź both as soft zh, as in *seizure*

ó as oo, as in boot

ą as a nasal, as in French *on*

ę as a nasal, as in French *en*

ł as w, as in *way*

ń as ny, as in *canyon*

The accent in Polish words always falls on the penultimate syllable.

Holy Week

Chapter 1 ‖|

JAN MALECKI HAD NOT seen Irena Lilien for quite some time. As late as the summer of 1941, they still had seen a good deal of each other. By that time, the Liliens had been driven out of their home in Smug; but the German occupation authorities were not yet taking harsher measures against the Jews, so the Liliens, having paid off the necessary people, had avoided confinement in the Warsaw Ghetto. They had even managed to rescue some of their things, and with this remainder of their belongings, still quite sizable and valuable, the entire family moved closer to Warsaw.

The Liliens, who before the war had been people of means—and for several generations, at that—were possessed of such a deeply developed sense of security that, even in the new and critical situation in which they now found themselves, it did not occur to them to move to a different suburb. Zalesinek, where they rented an apartment, was located about a quarter of the way to Smug, and many people along the commuter line knew the Liliens, whether personally or by sight. They had become so much a part of Polish culture and customs that they had no idea they might arouse suspicion by their outward appearance.

Fortunately, the oldest generation of Liliens, the banker and his wife, did not travel to Warsaw. She, an immense, fat Jewish woman, had been incapacitated for a number of years and never left her wheelchair. Her husband, long ago having withdrawn from affairs at the bank, contented himself by sitting in the sun or, on rainy or cold days, by watching people play bridge. But his son Professor Lilien, his wife, and their daughter, Irena, still traveled to Warsaw as often as before. Mrs. Lilien attracted relatively little attention. Small, slender, and quiet, with irregular but pleasant features, she could pass for Aryan. It was much worse for the professor and Irena.

Irena went into Warsaw several times a week. She visited friends and acquaintances—and a desire to see Malecki occasioned other trips as well. She loved her social life and an atmosphere of fun; she liked to arrange meetings in the bars and cafés that were so fashionable during the war. Irena Lilien was very pretty: tall, dark-haired, and dark-complexioned. Her coarse, thick hair and eastern eyes, however, were strikingly Jewish. When Malecki explained that she ought to be more careful, Irena just laughed and said that the Germans knew nothing of such things. Of course, at that time, incidences of extortion by Poles already had begun to occur, but Irena did not take seriously the possibility of such a thing ever happening to her or to those close to her. Her beauty, and the social position to which she had been born and to which she had become accustomed, lent her a sense of security from all danger.

Professor Lilien, for other reasons, having more to do with his upbringing, likewise did not take seriously the possibility that anything could happen to him. The war had shaken him very badly. The triumph of bestiality over regard for human life put his innate humanity and liberalism to a hard test, but he emerged from it with an unswerving belief in life and in human progress. However, the defense of those threatened values cost him dearly. Juliusz Lilien, gifted with a remarkable historical intuition and imagination, was bereft of any imagination at all with regard to his own fate or that of those closest to him. There are people who, having attained a high position in society, cannot imagine the existence of any power capable of casting them down and depriving them of what they have achieved. Lilien was just such a person. Even after being driven from Smug and forced to exchange his luxurious and spacious villa[1] for three sublet rooms, deprived of his library, servants, and creature comforts, he remained in his sensibilities the same person he had been before the war: the scion of an old and wealthy family, a justly renowned historian, an oft-named university master and dean, and a member of various scholarly societies both in Poland and abroad. In the public mind, Lilien was reputed to be a Mason of some distinction, but whether he really was—and, if so, what role he might have played in the organization—would have been hard to say. He had influential relatives in all the countries of Europe and in America, as well as friends in academic circles, in international finance, and in politics. If he did not leave Poland after the September defeat and later failed to avail himself of the opportunity of travel to Italy, it was no doubt due primarily to his deep-rooted certainty that, through all of life's vicissitudes, he would remain

Professor Lilien. The first years of the war already had narrowed the scope of his activities and his significance but had not succeeded in altering his attitude. He worked incessantly, wrote and read, and visited those of his colleagues who remained in Warsaw. In his manner of living and in his thought and experience, he endeavored to affirm the rather illusory truth that the objective shape of the world and its events can be obliterated and pushed into the shadows by the interpretation one ascribes to things.

The Liliens spent the entire summer in Zalesinek, and Malecki visited them there several times. The neighborhood was typical of suburban Warsaw —barren and sandy, and crowded with ugly villas set among dwarfish pine trees. In comparison to beautiful Smug, charmingly set in the middle of an old park and ponds and surrounded by dense and abundant alders, blackthorns, and bird-cherries, Zalesinek was poor and sad-looking. The banality of the sublet apartment was ameliorated somewhat by the things the Liliens had brought with them from Smug, and there were still a good many books in the professor's room.

Malecki went to Zalesinek for the last time one Sunday in August. In addition to him, there was the young painter Fela Ptaszycka—nicknamed Birdie, despite her enormous stature—a friend of Irena's and an admirer of the intellectual virtues of the professor.[2] No other guests fulfilled their promise to come—a surprise, since on Saturday and Sunday many people usually visited the Liliens, and their expansive, two-story house in Smug would become as full as a boardinghouse or hotel. The Liliens had complained on occasion about the excess of guests, but they had become so used to it that they felt unpleasantly surprised by the lonely holiday. They served an excellent dinner, with chicken and a very elaborate dessert. But not even the purchase of French cognac from some German soldiers, which Irena poured into dark Turkish coffee, could set the awkward atmosphere aright. Although the professor was talkative, it seemed that his erudition and witty humor required numerous listeners to be truly effective. Irena was overly boisterous, laughing too much and too loudly. Ptaszycka carried within her massive body a tender and sensitive heart and, in her desire that a good mood prevail, time and again committed horrible social gaffes. That she did this so sincerely and with such evident goodwill only worsened the situation.

After dinner, wanting to be alone with Malecki at last, Irena proposed a walk in the direction of the old woods. But first the professor had to lay out for Malecki a picture of the political situation of the world at war; then Ptaszycka again interfered and when, after a long while, it finally dawned on her that she was in the way, she was unable to extricate herself from her awkward role. In the end, Malecki returned to Warsaw on an earlier train than usual. Irena announced her intention to travel to the city on the following Wednesday, but neither on that day nor on any of the following days was there any sign of her. In connection with his work on the renovation of a certain Cistercian monastery,[3] Malecki left for a remote province and visited Irena only after his return at the end of the following week.

During this time, the Liliens had encountered a number of unpleasant incidents. Someone must have informed on them, because on the Wednesday after that Sunday, the Gestapo[4] began to take an interest in them. This time, matters were much more serious. First, the professor himself was seized and detained at headquarters for a day and a night. The following morning, the same agents came and transported Mrs. Lilien and Irena to the Warsaw Ghetto. They were there for only a few hours, and the professor too was released; but this time, as Irena related, it was evident that the ransom for his freedom had been very high. Of course, staying in Zalesinek was now out of the question. It was vital that they leave immediately and take with them only the most essential of their belongings.

The biggest problem was with the elder Liliens, the banker and his wife. Finally, after long deliberations and overcoming many and various obstacles, both were placed in a private clinic in Warsaw. The professor left for Kraków to survey conditions there, while his wife stayed with her distant family, which up to that point had been safe. Irena was taken in by Fela Ptaszycka. Shortly thereafter, within a very short interval, the elder Liliens both passed away. The professor returned from Kraków less vibrant than usual, nothing apparently having come of his plans. Only now did the Liliens decide to take out Aryan papers[5] for themselves. Under the name of Grabowski, they settled once again on the outskirts of Warsaw, this time on the right bank of the Vistula, along the railway line toward Otwock. But two weeks later, when they barely had settled in, they had to move again hurriedly, changing location almost from hour to hour.

Malecki saw the Liliens for the last time at Fela Ptaszycka's. He found that the professor had changed the most. He was depressed, he looked very old, and he was unshaven and sloppily dressed. The unkemptness only underscored his Semitic appearance. He now closely resembled his dead father, who in his old age had looked unmistakably Jewish. Mrs. Lilien, likewise, looked the worse for her experiences and was even quieter and more withdrawn than usual. Only Irena was holding up well, as she attempted to turn the situation into a joke or some adventure that would certainly end both soon and favorably. Her nervous, restless gaiety was even harder to take than her parents' depression. Collectively, they did not know what to do with themselves. Ptaszycka lived in Saska Kępa[6] in her mother's villa, and, despite her best intentions, she could not keep Irena with her for more than a week, two at most. The Lilien family had fallen into unforeseen difficulties. The professor was lodging for the time being with one of his students, but this arrangement was not permanent. From what the professor said, one could guess that he had been disappointed by many people on whose help he had counted. It seemed that, for him, this blow was the most painful of all. He felt at once vulnerable and powerless. As the three sat in Ptaszycka's studio on that sunny spring afternoon, drinking tea out of beautiful English porcelain, they seemed like hopelessly sad and dismal castaways with no place to turn.

|||

A few weeks later, Malecki received a letter from Irena. She wrote from Kraków. By this time, Jan had become absorbed in important matters of a personal nature, and then he had to leave again for the Cistercian monastery; and so, not having answered her letter immediately, he did not answer it at all. After that, one more letter arrived from Irena, short and very sad, and in its tone not at all like her usual self. This time he wanted to answer, but the aforementioned affairs had so distanced him from Irena that he did not know what to say. He saw that Irena was unhappy, lonely, and that her life was going badly. He, by contrast, was happy. Despite all the wartime calamities, he was beginning a new life, and there is among people no dividing line greater or more absolute than that between the happiness of some and the suffering of others. Affairs great and small divide people, yet none so sharply as the inequality of fate.

By the time his marriage with Anna was finalized, the figure of Irena had receded into a far corner of Malecki's thoughts, and neither sympathy for her situation nor the remnants of their former friendship were enough to prompt him to reach out to her. Finally, Irena stopped writing. For a time, Fela

Ptaszycka still had news of her, but later even that broke off. Malecki visited his Cistercians a few more times, each time stopping en route in Kraków, but his attempts to look Irena up ended only with good intentions. In the summer of 1942, when the Germans began liquidating the ghettos and organizing the mass slaughter of Jews throughout the country, rumors spread about the death of Professor Lilien. But different versions circulated, and it was difficult to verify how much truth there was to them.

It was not until spring of the following year that Malecki unexpectedly, and amid quite special circumstances, met Irena again. It was the Tuesday before Easter.

Chapter 2 ‖ı

I T   W A S   A   G L O O M Y Holy Week for Warsaw. Just the day before Malecki's encounter with Irena, on Monday the nineteenth of April, some of the Jews still remaining in the ghetto had begun to defend themselves against new German repressions. In the early morning, as SS[1] detachments moved inside the ghetto walls, the first shots rang out on Stawki and Leszno streets. The Germans, who had not expected any resistance, withdrew. The battle had begun.

News of the first collective Jewish resistance in centuries did not immediately get about the city. Various versions circulated around Warsaw. In the first hours it was known only that the Germans intended to liquidate the ghetto once and for all and to kill all the Jews who had survived the previous year's massacres.

The neighborhoods bordering the walls swarmed with people, for there it was easiest to find out what was happening. One after another, shots rang out from the windows of the apartment houses adjoining the walls. The Germans brought their military police up to the ghetto. Hour after hour, the intensity of the gunfire increased. The defense, at first chaotic and random, quickly assumed the shape of a regular organized resistance. Machine-gun fire rang out in many places, and grenades flew.

Street traffic still functioned normally, and in many places the conflict took place amid a throng of spectators and the rattle of passing streetcars. At the same time, the remaining Jews were being taken away from those neighborhoods where no resistance had been raised. Few realized on that first day that the destruction of the ghetto would be drawn out for many long weeks. But for as many days as the Jews defended themselves, the ghetto would continue to burn. And so it was, amid the springtime atmosphere of Holy Week, in the heart of Warsaw, which four years of terror had been unable to subdue, that the Jewish insurrection got under way, the loneliest and most agonizing of all the struggles undertaken in those times in defense of life and freedom.

Malecki lived on the edge of Bielany, a distant settlement on the northern part of town. It was as he returned home from work on Monday evening that he first encountered the uprising. Just past Krasiński Square, as the streetcar passed along the walls of the ghetto, one could sense an atmosphere of excitement. People pressed up against the windows, but nothing could be seen. Beyond the ghetto ramparts stretched the high gray walls of tenement houses, cut through here and there by narrow windows, like arrow slits. Suddenly on Bonifraterska Street, in front of Saint John the Divine Hospital, the streetcar came to a violent stop. Simultaneously, from somewhere high up, a short, even burst of rifle fire rang out. A machine gun responded from the street.

Panic broke out in the streetcar. People quickly pulled back from the windows. Some squatted on the floor, while others pushed forward toward the exit. In the meantime, shots rained down more and more heavily from the Jewish apartment buildings. A machine gun set up in the middle of the pavement at the intersection of Bonifraterska and Konwiktorska streets answered with a ferocious chatter. Along the narrow stretch of roadway between the streetcar tracks and the walls of the ghetto an ambulance rushed by.

The next day, the streetcar to Żoliborz went only as far as Krasiński Square. Malecki, having completed his work at the firm more quickly than usual, was returning home early in the afternoon. At that moment, streetcar traffic came to a halt, and Miodowa Street was clogged with abandoned cars. Crowds stretched out along the sidewalks.

After a night of gunfire, with the morning came a short interruption in the fighting. Now, however, the pounding began anew, more ferocious than on the previous day. No vehicles were allowed to pass through Krasiński Square, but a restless, noisy, and excited crowd filled the openings of Długa and Nowiniarska streets. As with all major happenings in Warsaw, when observed from the outside it was something of a spectacle. Residents of Warsaw eagerly join a fight and just as eagerly observe one in progress.

A swarm of young boys and coiffed and elegantly dressed girls came running from the streets of the Old Town. The more curious pushed forward into the center of Nowiniarska Street, from which the most extensive view of the ghetto walls could be had. Hardly anyone pitied the Jews. The populace was mainly glad that the despised Germans were now beset by a new worry. In the estimation of the average person on the street, the very fact that fighting was taking place with a handful of solitary Jews made the victorious occupiers look ridiculous.

The fighting became increasingly fierce. In the heart of Krasiński Square, military policemen and SS guards bustled about in front of the judicial building. No one was allowed onto Bonifraterska Street.

When Malecki found himself at the corner of Miodowa Street, he was passed by an enormous truck loaded with soldiers dressed in full combat gear. Laughter broke out among the crowd, as rifle fire continued without interruption. This was the Jews shooting. The Germans responded with a long volley from their heavy machine guns and automatics.

Malecki had a business matter to take care of in the district bordering the field of battle, so he joined the crowd stretched out along Nowiniarska Street. The first stretch of this narrow street, badly damaged during the war, was separated from the ghetto walls by apartment house blocks standing between Bonifraterska and Nowiniarska streets, which ran parallel to each other. A short distance away, beyond the first cross street—Świętojerska—the buildings came to an end, and the street opened onto a vast, empty, and potholed square that had come into being after the razing of buildings bombed out and burned during the siege of Warsaw.

At the point where Nowiniarska opened upon this square, the crowd thickened, and the sidewalks and roadway became packed with people. Only a few strayed beyond the square. Shots could still be heard from the direction of the Jewish houses. In the intervals when the shooting died down, people broke away from the crowd a few at a time and vanished in haste beneath the walls of the apartment buildings.

Just as Malecki reached a place exposed to fire from the insurgents, the shooting came to a halt, and people, some hurrying home or on errands and others driven by curiosity, pushed forward in a thick wave. The deserted square now seemed even wider. In its center stood two carousels not yet completely assembled, evidently being readied for the upcoming holiday. Under the cover of their wildly colored decorations stood helmeted German soldiers. A number of them were kneeling on the platform with rifles pointed toward the ghetto. The area beneath the ghetto walls was empty. Above them, heavy and silent, rose the high walls of the apartment buildings. With their narrow windows and broken rooflines set against the cloudy sky, they recalled the image of a huge fortress.

Emboldened by the calm, people began to stop and to survey the solitary walls. Suddenly, shots rang out from that direction. Farther along Bonifraterska Street, probably near St. John the Divine Hospital, a deafening explosion could be heard, and many more followed, one after another. The Jews must have been throwing grenades.

People quickly began to take cover in the nearby entryways as shots whistled through the air. One of the running men, a stocky little fellow in a straw hat, gave a shout and fell onto the sidewalk. In the square a machine gun was stuttering. The soldiers at the carousel also were firing. Simultaneously, a series of sharp and very powerful shots rocked the square, and a streak of silvery shells struck one of the highest windows of the defended houses. It was an antitank gun firing in response.

In the ensuing havoc, Malecki found himself far from the closest gate, and he instinctively retreated into the doorway of the first store at hand. The storefront was boarded over, but the recess was deep enough to afford a measure of protection.

The street had nearly emptied. Two broad-shouldered workers were lifting the man lying on the sidewalk. One of them, a younger man, also picked up the straw hat. A soldier standing by the wall urged them to hurry. Then, gesticulating violently, he shouted loudly in the direction of a woman who, alone among the passersby, remained on the street. She stood motionless on the edge of the sidewalk and, as if unaware of the danger to which she was exposing herself, stared straight ahead at the dark walls.

"Don't stand there, miss!" cried Malecki.

She did not even turn around. It was not until the soldier leaped up, screaming and shoving her away, that she stepped back and cradled her head in her arms in an uncertain gesture of surprise and fear. The soldier, exasperated and angry, pushed her with the butt of his rifle toward the gate. At the same time, he saw Malecki hidden in the recess of the store.

"*Weg! Weg!*" he screamed at him.

Malecki jumped out and quickly ran after the fleeing woman. Shots now came from all sides. A volley of shells rang out from a small antitank gun in the square. Glass flew tinkling onto the sidewalk. Again the dull explosion of grenades was heard.

The woman and Malecki reached the gate almost simultaneously. It was closed, and before it opened, Malecki finally was able to get a look at his companion, still hunched over and frightened, but whose profile was now turned toward him. The moment he saw her, he gasped in amazement.

"Irena!"

She looked at him with dark, uncomprehending eyes.

"Irena!" he repeated.

At the same moment, the frightened young doorkeeper opened the gate. "Faster! Faster!" she urged.

Malecki grabbed Irena by the hand and yanked her inside. The entryway was filled with people, so he pushed his way through the crowd toward the courtyard. Irena allowed herself to be led, obediently and without resistance. He pulled her deeper into the courtyard, where it was empty.

The courtyard was old, dirty, and very run down. In place of what had once been an annex rose an empty plaster-specked wall, a remnant of wartime devastation. In the middle was a tall stack of bricks, alongside which lay a gray patch of poor barren earth, evidently prepared for planting vegetables.

As they came to a stop next to a steep set of stairs leading to the basement, Malecki let go of Irena's hand and took a closer look at her.

She was still beautiful, but very changed. She had grown thin, and her features had become sharper and more subtle. Her oval eyes had become somehow even larger, but their expression had lost the warm color that had been so characteristic of her. They were now foreign, almost raw. Irena was very well dressed.

She wore a light-blue wool suit brought over from England before the war and a becoming hat, which Malecki did not recognize. Whether because he had not seen her for a long time or whether the changes were real, at first glance she now seemed to Malecki even more Semitic than before.

"It's you?" she said quickly and without surprise.

Her eyes gave him a careless once-over. She seemed still to be listening to the sounds of gunfire from the street.

Malecki pulled himself together.

"Where did you come from? What are you doing here? You're in Warsaw?"

"Yes," she answered matter-of-factly, as if they had parted just a short time ago.

Her voice was the same as before, low and resonant, but perhaps somewhat less vibrant, a bit flat.

"How long have you been here?"

Irena shrugged.

"Oh, I don't know. I don't even remember exactly. It seems like a very long time."

"And you didn't let me know?"

She looked at him more closely and a trifle mockingly.

"What for?"

Malecki lost his composure. This simple question was completely unexpected, so unlike the Irena he had known before. Not knowing what to say, he fell silent. Irena was listening again to the din from the street, and in her strained, somewhat distraught and frightened focus, she seemed to have forgotten about her companion. The silence became prolonged and increasingly uncomfortable and burdensome for Malecki. He felt a clear sense of estrangement from Irena, and in view of the situation in which she now found herself, he very much wanted to erase the distance between them but did not know how.

In the meantime, voices could suddenly be heard in the entryway. Part of the crowd hurriedly began to withdraw into the courtyard. A little boy in torn pants and a ragged shirt flew through the entrance and, knocking against Malecki in his haste, shouted excitedly down into the basement:

"Mama! They've set up a gun in our gate! They're going to shoot from our gate!"

Brushing back a flaxen strand of hair that had fallen across his forehead, he ran back to the gate. A pale and wasted woman leaned out of the basement.

"Rysiek! Rysiek!" she called after the child.

But he was no longer there. Walking heavily, the woman lumbered up the steep and uncomfortable stairs. Suddenly an antitank gun began to fire. A deafening series of booms rattled the walls. From somewhere on an upper story plaster sifted down.

"Oh, Lord!" cried the woman, clutching at her heart.

The gun pounded without interruption. Everything about trembled and quaked, while the shooting from the Jewish side had grown quiet. And in this deafening uproar there mingled the sound of a raspy phonograph from the next courtyard playing some kind of sentimental prewar tango. More and more people withdrew from the gate.

"Oh, Lord!" the woman from the basement repeated wearily. "For what sins must we suffer so?"

Irena, trembling and pale from the strain of the gunfire, roused herself to respond to this complaint.

"Those people over there are suffering more," she said hostilely.

Her eyes flashed and her mouth was tightly clenched. Malecki had never seen such malice and bitter antagonism in her.

The woman raised her tired, faded eyes to Irena.

"More? And how do you know what I have suffered?"

"Over there people are dying," Irena cut her off in the same hostile voice.

"Drop it . . ." Malecki whispered.

But Irena, unable to control herself, turned on him viciously.

"Why should I? People are dying over there, hundreds of people, and you, over here, are letting them die like dogs . . . worse than dogs."

She raised her voice and became much more agitated. Malecki grabbed for her hand and pulled her aside toward the entry to one of the stairwells.

"Get hold of yourself! You're looking for trouble. Think about what you're doing—people are already beginning to stare at us."

As a matter of fact, several people who had drawn back from the gates were peering curiously in their direction. Irena looked around. Perceiving their glances, she immediately calmed down and fell silent.

"My papers are in order," she whispered timidly.

She anxiously looked Malecki in the eyes.

It made him uncomfortable, as never before in his entire acquaintance with Irena. He was terribly embarrassed and humiliated by her situation and by his own helplessness and privileged position.

"What are you talking about?" he blurted out somewhat artificially. "No one is going to look at your papers now. The worst thing is that there's no way of knowing when we can get out of here. Where are you living?"

"Nowhere."

Malecki shuddered.

"What do you mean nowhere?"

"Just as I say."

"But you said you've been in Warsaw for a while."

"For a while, but what of it? I can't go back to where I was living. But no matter," she said disdainfully, "it's not important."

"How is it not important? Listen, what about your father?"

She looked at him briefly.

"He's dead."

"So it's true?" he whispered. "There were rumors to that effect . . ."

"It's true."

He was silent for a while. Finally, forcing himself, he asked:

"And your mother?"

"She's dead too."

It was the answer he had expected, but as soon as he heard it, he felt its full weight upon him.

"That's terrible!" was all he managed to say.

And he immediately felt how meaningless his words were. But Irena, standing with her head bowed and tracing invisible patterns in the broken asphalt with the end of her brown parasol, did not convey the impression that she was expecting anything else from him. Her suffering had become so deeply embedded that she expected from others neither compassion nor warmth.

Malecki looked distractedly at the movements of Irena's parasol. More keenly than usual he felt the same onrush of emotion that inevitably took root of its own accord whenever he contemplated the increasingly frequent tragedies of the Jews. These feelings were different from those that arose within him for the suffering of his own compatriots and of the people of other nations. They were dark, complex, and deeply disturbing. At the moments of their greatest intensity, they became entangled in an especially painful and humiliating awareness of a hazy and indistinct sense of responsibility for the vastness of the atrocities and crimes to which the Jewish people had been subjected now for many years, while the rest of the world silently acquiesced. That awareness, stronger than any intellectual reasoning, was probably the worst experience he had taken from all his wartime encounters. There were times, as at the end of the previous summer, when the Germans had first begun the mass slaughter of the Jews and when for days and nights on end the Warsaw Ghetto had resounded with the sounds of shooting, that his feelings of complicity became exceptionally strongly aroused. He bore them then like a wound in which there seemed to fester all the evil of the world. He realized, however, that there was within him more unease and terror than actual love toward these defenseless people, who now found themselves cornered on all sides, the only people in the world whom fate had uprooted from a demeaned, but still existing, human brotherhood.

The present encounter with Irena only heightened Malecki's confusion, which had been growing within him since the previous evening. He had felt very depressed then because, as a typical man of education, he was the kind of person who finds it easy enough to relate the sufferings and cruelties of all mankind to his own pangs of conscience.

In the meantime, the antitank gun fell silent. From the phonograph in the neighboring courtyard now rose the ringing voice of a male tenor. Round and resonant words of Italian floated loudly and clearly about the walls of the ghetto. Machine guns rattled from the middle of the square. The people who had retreated to the courtyard now returned to the gate. The same small boy, whose mother had called him Rysiek, burst from the entryway and ran up to the woman, still standing by the stairs to the basement.

"Mama! The Germans are blowing up the Jews' houses! Oh, look what huge holes they've already made!" he said, holding his hands wide apart.

"Go home, Rysiek!" the woman whispered.

He shook his unruly, dirty-blond hair.

"I'll be right back."

Turning on his heels, he ran back to the entryway.

"Maybe now we can go back out on the street." Malecki said, and left Irena to see what was happening at the gate.

He saw an artillery piece standing in front of the building and several German soldiers around it. The machine gun rattled constantly from the middle of the square. The gate was half open. A small group of people was negotiating with a tall, broad-shouldered soldier to allow them to exit. The soldier at first did not want to let them out, but at last he stepped aside and waved them past. Instantly several dozen people darted toward the exit.

Malecki swiftly returned to Irena.

"Listen, we can leave, but quickly, because they'll probably start up again soon."

Looking at Irena, he fell silent. She was pale and her face had changed. She leaned on one hand against the wall of the building.

"What's the matter?" he asked, frightened. "Do you feel sick?"

"No," she protested.

But she grew even paler. Malecki looked around and quickly approached the woman from the basement.

"May I ask you for some water? This woman is feeling faint."

The woman looked at Irena and hesitated for a moment. Finally she nodded her head.

"Follow me."

Malecki descended after her and stopped at the door. The odor of poverty struck him immediately. In the basement was a kitchen nook, low-ceilinged, darkened with soot, and saturated with dampness. There was hardly any furniture. On a wooden bed next to the wall lay an old and emaciated man, covered with the remnants of a once-red quilt. Nearer the entrance, a dark young man sat on a stool, peeling potatoes. The work went amazingly quickly. With machinelike speed his pocketknife flashed, and with measured motions he deftly tossed the peeled potatoes into a basin of water on the floor. The young man was leaning downward into the shadows; his face could not be made out.

The woman drew some water from a bucket and handed a mug to Malecki. He thanked her and quickly returned upstairs to Irena.

"Have some of this," he said, offering her the water.

At first she did not want to take it, but finally she allowed herself to be persuaded. After a couple of swallows she pushed the mug aside.

"I can't," she whispered with revulsion.

She was slowly regaining her composure, but she still trembled slightly and kept leaning against the wall.

"How do you feel?"

She nodded, feeling better. At that moment the woman emerged from the basement.

"Maybe the lady would like to sit down?" she called. "Let her come downstairs."

Malecki looked inquiringly at Irena. To his surprise, she agreed, and he led her down the stairs. The woman wiped off a wooden stool with a rag.

"Please have a seat," she told Irena and placed the stool nearer the door.

Malecki stood beside her. The antitank guns began to sound again. The man lying next to the wall began to moan, but the woman paid him no attention. She stood before the kitchen, thin and frail, with her arms hanging down, clearly tired beyond endurance. Although she wore a miserable threadbare dress, she looked well-enough groomed. Her hair, already graying, was smoothly combed, revealing the sallow skin of her temples, transparent as vellum. She must have been no more than forty years old, although she looked much older.

Malecki glanced toward the bed.

"Is that your husband? Is he sick?"

"He's sick," she replied. "But he's not my husband. He's my husband's father."

"And your husband?"

"He was killed in September."[2]

Irena only now looked about the room. The woman immediately noticed her glance.

"The Germans threw us out of Poznań province," she explained. "We had a little house in Mogilno. My husband was a gardener there."

She fell silent and looked about the place herself.

"And now—it's all gone!"

Malecki, who had been watching the young man peel potatoes for some time, could no longer restrain himself and exclaimed:

"You're really good at that!"

The youth started, broke off his work, and raised his head. His face, which once must have been gentle and not bad-looking, now was swollen, and the livid, brick-colored spots on his cheeks gave the impression of a mask. His hair was cropped close to the skin, his eyelids deeply red, and his eyes dead, motionless, and without luster. His glassy stare, so little resembling anything human, had a crushing effect on Malecki. He was relieved when the boy, without responding, again bent over and, taking another potato from the small basket, began to peel it skillfully with his red and slightly swollen hands.

No one spoke. The man moaning next to the wall attempted to pull his hands out from under the scraps of quilt. The tenor on the phonograph in the courtyard began singing a new aria. From far away, the short reports of single shots rent the air.

At that, the woman spoke up.

"That's my oldest son, just returned from Auschwitz."[3]

No one said anything in reply. The woman looked at her son with a tired gaze, while he continued indifferently, as if no one had said anything about him.

"He was there for two years. They caught him on the street."

Abruptly she began bustling about the kitchen, shifting around dented pots and saucepans. There was no fire burning in the stove, and the cold was even more penetrating in the basement than outside. The sun certainly never shone here.

Malecki glanced at Irena. She had completely returned to normal, although she was a bit paler than usual. She sat rigid and attentive, unnaturally straight, her dark eyes examining the woman attentively but with an evident lack of goodwill. The woman, for her part, finally stopped rearranging things, turned, and went up to her son.

"Enough peeling, Kaziczek," she said gently. "That'll do for today."

At that moment the shrill, hoarse shout of one of the soldiers rang out from in front of the gate. The young man started, moved away from the window, and instinctively shrank into himself. For a moment, his red eyes passed across Malecki and Irena with an apprehensive squint. Only when he saw his mother did he calm down somewhat. He continued standing alone, lurking in the corner and gazing uncertainly at the strangers in the room.

"Let's go!" Malecki leaned over to Irena. She stood up with some effort and thanked the woman, indifferently and with a trace of contempt, for her hospitality.

This cut Malecki to the quick.

"Irena!" he said, his voice rising with reproach, "How can you speak to these unfortunate people in that tone of voice?"

She glanced at him with the same derisive coldness as at the beginning of their encounter.

"So you don't like my tone of voice?"

"No."

The hardness in his own voice did not disconcert her at all.

"Too bad. That's the tone I seem to have."

"But Irena!"

"What are you so surprised at?" she asked, cutting him off irritatedly. "That woman is not the unhappiest person in the world. She doesn't have to die from the fear that at any moment they can shoot her sons just because they are who they are. She at least has them, you understand? She can go on living. And us?"

"Us?" He didn't understand at first.

"Us Jews!" she answered.

At that moment, the sound of a machine gun sounded very close to them. The cannon continued firing from the far gate.

"You didn't used to say 'us,'" Malecki said at last, speaking softly.

"No, I didn't, but I have been taught. By all of you."

"By us?"

"By you, Poles, Germans . . ."

"So you're lumping us together?"

"You're all Aryans!"

"Irena!"

"You taught me that. I only recently came to understand that everyone in the world has always hated us and still does."

"You're exaggerating!" he murmured.

"Not at all! And even if they don't hate us, at best they barely tolerate us. Don't tell me we have friends, because it just seems that way. In reality no one likes us. Even when you help us, it's different than when you help other people . . ."

"Different?"

"You have to force yourself to assume a posture of generosity and sympathy, of whatever is good, humane, and just. Oh, I assure you that if I could hate Jews as much as you do, then I wouldn't say 'us' and 'you.' But I can't feel like that and so I must be one of them, a Jew! For who else am I supposed to be, tell me that?"

"Yourself," he replied, but without much conviction.

She said nothing at first. She bowed her head and stood that way for a long time, again tracing invisible signs on the ground with her parasol. Suddenly she lifted her beautiful, eastern eyes toward Malecki and said in the soft tone that formerly had so often sounded in her voice:

"I am myself. But Miss Lilien from Smug no longer exists. I was told to forget about her, so I did."

A commotion arose at the gate. People were slipping out, taking advantage of the latest break in the shooting.

"Let's go," Malecki said.

The German sentry at the gate urged those exiting to hurry. In a moment Malecki and Irena found themselves on the street.

Irena did not know this part of town, so she stopped, disoriented. Malecki pulled her after him in the direction of Franciszkańska Street. A few passersby were stealing this way along the rows of tenements. Shots still could be heard, sparse and far off. An open army car slowly made its way down the center of the roadway. From its running board a young officer issued orders in a loud voice to the soldiers grouped around the carousel.

Malecki and Irena had not yet reached Franciszkańska Street when shots
again began to ring out from the ghetto houses. The antitank gun answered
immediately. A trail of gleaming shells struck one of the lower windows.

Malecki quickened his pace.

"Faster! Faster!" he urged Irena.

By the time they got to Franciszkańska Street, a thick, brick-colored
cloud was obscuring the shelled-out window. Columns of smoke billowed
out, looking at first like an ordinary house fire. Meanwhile, shots rang out
from the other windows. A burst of machine-gun fire issued from the corner
of Franciszkańska.

A little farther up Franciszkańska stood a small group of people, safely
observing the battle. A stocky boy in lime-besmirched overalls nudged his
friend:

"Heniek, look! You see the dead Jew?"

"Let's go," Malecki whispered.

Irena stopped and looked in the direction the stocky boy had indicated.
Sure enough, in one of the windows already annihilated by shells one could
see a corpse hanging across the windowsill. The dead man's head and arms
hung out the window. From that distance he appeared quite small, almost unlike a human being.

"You see?" the boy asked his comrade.

"Yeah," the other answered. "He's hanging up there real good, isn't he?"

At the news that a dead Jew could be seen, people began to gather and
stare. At one point a small, frail woman carrying a large basket loaded with
spinach and radishes pushed through the crowd.

"Where? Where?" she began to ask, squinting. "I can't see a thing."

"There, straight ahead!" a ragged old cigarette vendor informed her.
"Just follow my finger."

Beyond the crowd, and a little to one side, a boy of perhaps sixteen stood
leaning against the wall of a ruined apartment building. He was dark, slender,
and dressed in a windbreaker. Malecki knew the boy well by sight. It was his
neighbor from Bielany, Włodek Karski, who lived with his mother and sister
in the same house as the Maleckis. Włodek's father, a major in the army, was
a prisoner in Germany. Because of their proximity (the Karskis lived on the
floor above), young Karski had impressed Malecki as a graceless youth somewhat inclined to acts of foolishness. He and the numerous acquaintances he

was constantly bringing home with him made a racket on the stairs and in the apartment with their hobnailed boots. Now as he stood there, pale and with his brows set in an angry frown, he looked unexpectedly grown up. Only in his tightly clenched teeth was there still a trace of a childish grimace of anger.

In the meantime the assembled people had had their fill of looking at the corpse hanging from the window. Only the woman with the spinach and radishes was not able to make it out.

"Where? Where?" she kept asking insistently, squinting her nearsighted eyes.

Someone finally grew annoyed.

"Take your eye out, lady. Maybe you'd see better that way," he said.

Guffaws broke out among the crowd. Malecki drew closer to Irena and took her by the arm.

"Let's get out of here, Irena!"

At the same moment, as shots rang closer, the crowd began to disperse. At last Irena allowed Malecki to take her away, into the depths of Franciszkańska Street. She still kept turning around to look.

"Don't look back there any more!" he muttered impatiently. "What's the point?"

They walked along the sidewalk in silence, pressed in on all sides by the throng and the uproar. New groups of people, curious to see the field of battle from up close, kept arriving from the direction of Old Town. The cannonade beneath the walls was now unleashed in full force. Echoes of the shots resounded among the tightly crammed together buildings. From the roofs, balconies, and recesses pigeons violently flew up and fluttered above the street. A pair of young men raced down the street on noisy scooters. The sky was cloudy. It was cold and windy, though it still smelled of spring.

At the end of Franciszkańska Street, before arriving at the Franciscan church near Fret Street, Irena stopped.

"Where are we? What am I going here for?"

"What do you mean 'what for'?" Malecki asked in surprise. "You're coming to stay with us."

And then he asked:

"You probably didn't know I got married?"

"Yes, I know," she answered curtly.

"From Fela Ptaszycka?"

"Yes."

They stood at the intersection of Franciszkańska and Fret, alongside a booth with marigolds and bouquets of primroses. Large numbers of people continued walking along both streets. The crowd and the hum of voices completely changed the usual sheltered and quiet atmosphere of the old neighborhood.

Malecki withdrew from the edge of the sidewalk.

"Well?"

By the expression on Irena's face, it seemed as though she was hesitating and did not exactly know what to do.

"Do you have any place else to go?" he asked.

"Not at the moment, no."

"So, what are you waiting for? It's as simple as that."

However, she stayed rooted to the spot.

"You think so?"

Malecki felt that he somehow had to simplify the decision for her. But since every good deed, when done more from a sense of obligation than from a genuine human response, requires inner effort, Malecki now had to try to overcome his selfish hesitation. As frequently happens to people in similar circumstances, he masked his internal indecision with an exaggerated heartiness. He remembered what Irena had said earlier, and it was important to him that she not sense in his invitation a trace of compulsion. But the more sincerely he explained why she ought to agree, the more strongly he felt the inequality of their situations. He came to realize that people generally aid others only when they themselves expect to feel rewarded.

Irena listened absentmindedly to Malecki's words, while carefully and attentively examining the expression on his face. Finally, disconcerted and a little irritated by her probing glance, he stopped speaking. He was torn between impatience and resistance, and fell silent in midsentence.

Irena unexpectedly averted her eyes.

"Fine, I'll come!" she said, looking straight ahead. "Is it far?"

He calmed down at once.

"Pretty far!" he replied almost cheerfully.

The moment he heard the relaxed sound of his own voice, he felt uneasy, as if he had committed an indiscretion. Irena's suffering was not his own, and he felt that he had to be constantly on guard against his own reactions and words so as not to underscore unwittingly the differences in their respective situations.

Silence again fell between them. Time and again Malecki quickened his step, only to slow down immediately when he saw that that Irena was tired and having trouble keeping up with him. Suddenly he had the idea that his silence might raise doubts in her as to whether he might be regretting his decision. A moment later, he wondered whether that actually might be true. Perhaps he had indeed acted in haste? Did he have the right to expose Anna to this sort of danger? He quickly cast that particular doubt aside, but his uncertainty continued to deepen.

People in increasing numbers moved along the sidewalks and pavement of Fret Street and, farther on, along Zakroczymska, trying to make it to the streetcars. Because the ghetto fighting had interrupted service, the trolleys had been cut off in the northern part of town, where they shuttled back and forth. Their route passed the district next to the ghetto, where the unceasing sounds of gunfire could be heard.

Near the park, which stood on the grounds of the old forts of the Citadel, Irena was the first to speak:

"It's good that you got married. I was once rather infatuated with you, but it's good you didn't want to marry me."

Malecki remained silent, as Irena looked at him with a smirk.

"We don't bring people happiness. Except, of course, when we have money."

He spontaneously came to a stop.

"What bitterness you have inside you, Irena!"

"Bitterness?" she said, surprised. "Why do you say that? It's only the truth."

"But it's a very bitter truth."

"Only for us. Why on earth should it be bitter for you?"

But she now apparently wanted to cover up the unpleasant impression her words were making, because she quickly began asking Jan about his present activities, how he was living and making do. Malecki answered in fragments. For a year he had been working for a firm as a middleman buying and selling real estate and building lots. He also had a lot of work rather loosely connected with his architectural profession, so that his salary, taken together with his commissions, was not bad. It was enough to live on.

"Your wife doesn't work?" she asked."

"No."

At first he wanted to explain that until recently she had worked in the same company as he, but now, because she was soon expecting a child, she had quit. However, at the last moment he decided not to bring this up, and again he felt remorse for his lack of openness toward her.

"What about your Cistercians?" she asked.

He was glad she had remembered that work of his. Unfortunately he had not been to Grotnica since the summer of the preceding year. But because of a lack of adequate funds, he had to set aside for better times the remainder of the restoration and preservation work. He livened up, however, and enthusiastically began to tell her what he had done in the old cloister up till now.

"So you went through Kraków?" Irena asked suddenly.

He couldn't deny it, and the conversation, which had been going so well, fell apart.

Heading toward the streetcars, they approached the Muranów section of the ghetto, and the sounds of gunshots and the banging of machine guns reached them with increasing intensity. Evidently the hard-fought insurgent battle raged on in this part of the ghetto as well.

They walked in silence across an open area between a park turning a light green and the brick forts of the old Citadel. The ghetto apartment houses were already at a distance. A brisk cold wind buffeted them from behind, from the direction of the Vistula River.

"What's your wife's name?" Irena asked.

He started, a little surprised.

"Anna."

"It's a pretty name."

After a moment, as if wanting to speak just so as not to hear the sounds of the ongoing cannonade, she said:

"Your wife will certainly be surprised to see me."

"Oh, no!" he denied vehemently and with an exaggerated assurance. "I've told Anna a lot about you."

"Of course she won't be surprised," he repeated after a moment.

He was, of course, mistaken; this much even he knew. The last thing Anna could have expected was to meet Irena Lilien.

|||

Knowing that Jan was supposed to return home early, Anna was worried by his prolonged absence. But when Włodek Karski returned home and, with some exaggeration, excitedly told her what was happening downtown, she could not stay in the apartment any longer and headed toward the stop at the end of the streetcar line.

She arrived just as Malecki and Irena were getting off the overcrowded car. She spotted them at a distance and instantly concluded that the tall and beautiful woman accompanying her husband must be an acquaintance met by chance on the streetcar. She was certain that Jan, upon seeing her waiting at the edge of the road, would quickly take leave of the woman and make his way to her alone. But since she had already experienced long hours of disquiet and imagined the longed-for moment of meeting differently, this unexpected detail wiped away her momentary joy. All of her worries about Jan now seemed to her ridiculous and unnecessary.

In the meantime, a huge throng of people was rushing to get off the streetcar, and Anna lost sight of Jan among the crowd swarming about the stop. German trucks covered with tarpaulins were at that very moment rolling down the highway, raising clouds of white dust overhead.

The convoy was a long one. The flatbed trucks rumbled along one after the other, and several long minutes passed before the people waiting at the stop were able to cross the road.

Malecki had not expected Anna to come out to meet him. He walked along absorbed in conversation with Irena without looking around, and he would no doubt have passed right by his wife without noticing her if she had not beckoned to him. He came to a sudden halt.

"Oh, there's Anna!" he said to Irena.

His instinctive joy immediately dissipated, however, when he noticed that Anna was wearing an old polka-dot dress he did not like, and which, in her pregnancy, she had let out many times. Compared to the elegantly dressed Irena, she seemed poor and unkempt. He knew that Irena attached great importance to a woman's outer appearance and, being the type of person who looks for confirmation of his own feelings in others, he had wanted Anna to make the best possible impression on Irena. He immediately placed the blame for his disappointment squarely on his wife.

Unfortunately, he was unable to summon up any tenderness when his own ego was at stake.

They slowly approached Anna, who was clearly caught off guard.

"Have you been waiting long?" he asked.

She shook her head.

Malecki, as usual in awkward circumstances, attempted to conceal his displeasure by feigning an easy manner.

"I've brought you a guest!" he said in an artificially hearty tone. "This is Irena Lilien."

His wife raised her eyes to Irena's and lightly blushed.

"And this is Anna," he said, turning to Irena and gesturing.

The women shook hands in silence. Malecki took off his hat, for he suddenly felt very warm.

"Shall we go?"

They set off toward the house. The road along which they walked from the streetcar stop to the distant villa in which the Maleckis lived was sandy and entirely rural. On one side was a dark pine forest full of the twitter of evening birds, while on the other stood a row of tidy white houses. All the houses were similar to one another—cheerful-looking, bright, and separated by garden plots white with pear and cherry blossoms interspersed here and there with the pink of almond trees and the delicate green of young birches. Against the general quiet, the sound of children's voices could be heard. In some of the gardens the earth was dug up for planting. After a cloudy and windy day, it was clearing up, and the sky stretched into the west, light blue and springlike. The air smelled of freshly turned earth and spruce trees.

"I've never been here before," said Irena, glancing around. "It's nice."

She then took no further notice of her surroundings. She walked between the Maleckis, carefully placing her graceful feet in the sandy ground, lightly swinging her parasol with a more citified manner than one could have expected from a woman so thoroughly accustomed to the countryside. From time to time, ignoring what Malecki was saying about the fighting in the ghetto, she peered at Anna, who remained silent. Of course she could not help noticing she was pregnant.

Jan's wife was neither pretty nor stylish. Pregnancy had already deformed her petite silhouette, inflating the languid lines of her figure. She moved along rather clumsily, walking with legs wide straddled, but even so she bore her shapelessness so naturally that the state in which she found herself was not at all unbecoming to her. She had light hair shading toward gray, irregular, almost common features, a too-big mouth, and protruding cheekbones. The only pretty feature of her face was her eyes, which were brown, moist, and very warm.

The wooden houses and pine grove came to an end, and a field, green with young rye, began.

"Is it much farther?" Irena asked.

"It's not too much farther now," said Anna, speaking up for the first time. "It's right behind those other houses."

The houses stood on the other side of the field but covered only part of the horizon. In the west, the view opened up into the distance. Beyond that was only open countryside—meadows, a gray and as yet leafless patch of lindens and poplars, after that some cottages, and then, even farther away, the purple shadow of forests. There the sun was setting, large and red as if turning to face the wind. At the end of the field a quiet street began, with homes built in the style of traditional Polish manor houses. In front of each was a small garden surrounded by lilacs and acacias that had not yet blossomed. This street led to the house in which the Maleckis lived.

"When is your son due?" Irena unexpectedly asked Malecki.

The question took him by surprise.

"Why a son?"

"Don't you want a son?"

"Of course we do," he laughed out loud.

"So when?"

"In the middle of June," Anna clarified.

Irena fell to thinking.

"That's a terribly long time."

"Why do you say that?" Malecki exclaimed. "It's only two months, not even that much."

"Two months is a very long time," Irena responded.

Anna lightly touched her hand.

"Yes, two months really is a long time, nowadays . . . but one has to have faith," she said sincerely in her low, warm voice.

Irena gave a hollow laugh.

"But I don't have any! All I want is to go on living."

"In order to live one must have faith," Malecki interjected.

Irena looked at him mockingly.

"Just what am I supposed to have faith in?"

"In life," Malecki plowed on.

Irena sneered contemptuously.

"Oh yes, right!"

Malecki could restrain himself no longer. He stopped and exclaimed, as if he had discovered something remarkable:

"And you say you want to live? What is that, then, if not having faith in life?"

Irena shrugged and lightly raised her parasol.

"Faith in life?" she repeated. "Not at all! It's simply that the more one sees death all around, the more strongly one wants to live, that's all."

They all fell silent.

"Here's our house!" said Anna, motioning to a villa surrounded by young spruces. Two young boys and a dark-haired, dark-complexioned young girl who looked a lot like Włodek Karski were playing in front of the house. The little girl, Teresa Karski, stood to one side with her hands clasped behind her neck watching the two boys, up to their elbows in sand and mud, building a long wall out of pebbles, branches, and shards of glass.

"What are you boys making?" Anna asked, pausing next to them.

One of the young boys raised a chubby-cheeked, grimy face toward her.

"It's the ghetto!" he said, pointing to the wall with pride.

Major Karski's wife, slim and as dark-complexioned as her children, stood in the entryway talking with a stocky, rotund woman who examined Irena with squinting and unfriendly eyes as they passed by.

Irena must have noticed, for she asked on the stairs immediately afterward, "What's with that woman, the fat one downstairs? Does she live here?"

"Yes," answered Malecki, "on the bottom floor."

"What's her problem, do you know?"

Malecki shrugged.

"I have no idea. Her last name is Piotrowski. She has a husband younger than she is. She smuggles things . . . That's all I know."

Irena became lost in thought, but a moment later, when they were at the Maleckis' door, she returned to the topic.

"She didn't look at me in a very friendly way . . ."

Malecki thought so too, so he eagerly disagreed.

"You're imagining it!"

"You think so?" she said, glancing at him fleetingly. "Good! I wouldn't want you to have any trouble because of me."

Malecki became glum.

"Don't be so touchy!" he said, more harshly than he had intended.

Again he was assailed by doubts as to whether he had done the right thing by bringing Irena to his house. She looked Jewish, there was no doubt about it. But he had known her far too long to have a sense of the impression she might make on people seeing her for the first time.

Having settled Irena in the room they called Jan's study, Anna went to the kitchen to make supper. In the meantime Irena had laid her parasol on the table and slowly began to take off her hat. Suddenly, with her hands still raised above her head, she turned toward Jan who was standing nearby.

"Why are you staring at me like that?"

He remained silent for a moment, then finally said, "You honestly haven't changed a bit . . ."

Irena placed her hat beside the parasol and sat down on the edge of the table.

"But you have—a lot."

"Really?"

"Unfortunately, yes. You've gotten old and ugly . . . seriously!" she affirmed, seeing the disconcerted expression on his face. "I don't think I could ever fall in love with you now."

Malecki felt it best to turn the conversation into a joke.

"And did you ever?"

"Why of course I did!" she laughed out loud. "Surely you never thought otherwise?"

Malecki was rescued from having to reply by the doorbell. It was Włodek Karski.

His blue sport shirt emphasized the darkness of his skin and hair.

"Excuse me," he nodded. "Is Mr. Malecki here, I mean, Julek?"

Malecki was taken aback.

"My brother?"

He had had no news of Julek for many weeks. He had left for the provinces sometime in February, without saying where or why, as usual on some secret business he didn't care to describe more closely.

In the meantime Anna peered out from the kitchen. Seeing young Karski, she smiled.

"Oh, it's you, Włodek!"

"I've come to see Julek. May I come in?"

"He's washing up at the moment," Anna explained. "Come back in a little while."

"All right, but please tell Julek I was here."

He nodded in parting, and clattering with his hobnailed boots, ran upstairs.

Malecki followed his wife back into the small, bright kitchen.

"You didn't tell me anything about Julek's coming. How long ago?"

"Right after noon," she replied. "He's been asleep almost the whole time."

Julek's tall boots stood on the floor next to the sideboard, flawlessly gleaming, carefully polished after his trip. Jan sat down in the nearest chair, across whose arms Julek's military-style breeches had been carelessly thrown. His wool socks lay next to the boots on the floor.

Anna was cutting bread at the table.

"Did he say anything?" he asked after a while.

"Julek?" she smiled. "You know him. He returned almost too exhausted for words. He said everything was fine and went to bed. Now he's taking a shower."

In fact one could hear the hiss and splash of the shower from behind the wall separating the kitchen and the bathroom.

At that moment the shrill voice of Mrs. Piotrowski could be heard from down below:

"Wacek! Wacek!"

Wacek was her son.

Malecki sat leaning forward with his elbows against his knees. Finally he lifted his head.

"Listen, does it seem to you that Irena looks awfully Jewish?"

"No, not so very much . . ."

"But Jewish enough, right?"

"Actually yes. And she's very beautiful."

Malecki frowned.

"So much the worse! She calls more attention to herself because of it. I don't know whether it was a good idea to bring her here."

Anna straightened up and stopped cutting bread.

"I think it was," she replied after a moment.

However he needed more convincing.

"Are you saying that sincerely? Do you really mean it?"

Anna turned toward him.

"Do you really know me as little as that?"

A tone of reproach sounded in her voice.

He said nothing in response. From the bathroom Julek's merry whistling could be heard. It grated unpleasantly on Malecki's ears as he returned to the interrupted conversation.

"She has changed a lot."

"Irena?"

"She's harder to deal with now . . . You can't imagine how hard . . ."

Anna stopped to think.

"And how is she supposed to be?"

"You're right, of course," he agreed. "You know, she now considers herself to be a Jew?"

He was disappointed when she did not answer. He had begun this conversation with the intention of dragging Anna into his dilemma in order to justify what he had done. He was moral enough to feel a need for self-justification, but not so moral as not to need to seek it. He tried to judge deeds by their underlying intentions, but since he frequently found intentions self-contradictory, he could not always find a proper basis for judgment. It was a dark and slippery morass in which he became more and more entangled. That was how he felt now.

He stood up, and before he could suppress his irritation, the words escaped of their own accord:

"Why are you wearing that dress?" he asked, glancing at his wife harshly. "You look terrible in it."

From the beginning of their conversation Anna had expected he would say something like that. On the way to the streetcar she had thought about it. She knew Jan could not stand that miserable polka-dot dress; for that matter, she did not like it either, but she had left the house in such distress that she had entirely forgotten to change her clothes. Along the way, she had paused and considered whether she should return home and put on a different dress. But at just that moment she had heard the approaching streetcar, so it was too late to go back. She had deceived herself by erroneously believing that her feminine sense of the importance of feelings, as opposed to things, would be shared by the man she loved. Despite the best of intentions, love between two people often turns into a ritual of mutual misunderstanding.

"I'll go right now and change," she said calmly.

Before he was able to soften the harshness of his words, the door to the bathroom banged open loudly, and Julek immediately appeared in the kitchen, washed and refreshed but with his hair still wet. He was taller than his brother, and his borrowed pajamas were too short on him.

"You're home already!" he said, turning to Jan. "Hey, old man! How's it going?"

Malecki greeted him rather coolly.

"All right. And you?"

"As you see! You've got a great bathroom. Best shower I've ever had. The pajamas are yours, as you can probably see. I took them out of the closet. You're not sore, are you?"

"You'd better get dressed, because supper is about to be served."

"Great!" exclaimed Julek gladly. "I'm ravenous. I'll get dressed, but first let me take my things out of here."

He leaned down for his boots and socks and, as the motion caused his hair to fall in his face, he energetically brushed it back.

"I hope you'll put me up for a night or two?"

"Of course, Julek," Anna responded from next to the window. "What do you think?"

"Thanks. Till Thursday or Friday at the most. Do you have a cigarette?" he asked, turning to his brother.

Jan took out his cigarette case. Julek took one and lit it from the stove.

"So you'll be leaving again?" Jan asked.

"I don't know yet. I'll have to see."

Holding his boots and socks under the crook of his arm and keeping his cigarette glued to his lips, he gathered his trousers off the chair. As he went to throw them over his shoulder, a small, dark revolver popped out of them onto the floor.

Julek quickly leaned over, grabbed the weapon, and stuck it back into the pocket of his trousers. A blush spread across his face, darkening his already deeply tanned skin.

Anna did not notice, and Jan considered it best to let the incident pass without comment.

"Where will you put me?" Julek asked, still a bit flustered. "In the study?"

Anna thought for a moment.

"No, probably in the dining room, though you'll not be comfortable there."

"Nonsense! I'm comfortable anywhere."

"We have a guest in the study."

"Oho!" Julek said interestedly. "And who might that be?"

"You don't know her," said Jan.

"A woman?"

"Irena Lilien."

Julek, who had heard now and again about the Liliens and their place in Smug, whistled in surprise, but did not say anything. He was heading toward the door when Anna remembered about Włodek.

"Oh, Julek! Włodek Karski was here a moment ago asking for you."

Julek stopped.

"Włodek?" he wondered. "Dark-skinned, dark hair?"

"Yes, he lives here above us."

"I know you who mean!" he smiled, nodding his head.

If it weren't for this smile, clearly alluding to some connection between the two, Jan might have been able to cover his annoyance. But now he let himself go.

"I can see by your enthusiasm that you've undertaken the proper indoctrination of our youth."

Julek frowned and immediately adopted an aggressive tone.

"What of it? You think that's bad?"

"Yes."

"That's too bad. For you, of course"

Malecki turned nearly white with rage.

"Look, you're twenty-something years old, and you can do what you like . . ."

"I hope so!" Julek spat back.

"But you have to realize what kind of harm you're doing to boys like that Karski, dragging them into such things—" and he pointed to the place where the revolver had fallen.

"I don't know what you're talking about!" Julek snorted violently. "It's not just that! We're fighting for something greater, more ... oh ... why do I even bother talking to you? One thing I will say, though, is that it's a shame nobody ever, as you say, saw to your proper indoctrination when you were sixteen years old!"

"Yeah, sure!" put in Jan.

"I mean it! You would have had less time for your own problems and wouldn't have grown into such a ... a ..." He waved his socks in the air. "Oh, you can fill in the rest for yourself."

Malecki trembled, but hid his agitation behind a contemptuous glare.

"What do you know about me?"

"About you?" Julek rolled his eyes. "I know enough to be able to judge you. You, on the other hand, know too little about yourself, or too much. In the end I guess it amounts to the same thing."

Jan laughed ironically.

"I see you've taken up philosophy. Beautiful! No one can accuse you of being too modest."

Julek was hastening to reply when his gaze fell on his sister-in-law.

She was standing next to the table with her head lowered, her profile to both of them. The shadow of her lashes fell upon her cheek. She looked both thoughtful and sad.

Julek immediately calmed down. He threw his breeches further back on his shoulder and approached his brother.

"Don't be angry, old man! I didn't mean to rile you."

But Jan wasn't ready to give in so easily.

"It seems to me that you make a habit of doing things you don't mean to do."

Julek's mouth trembled, and his cheeks reddened. He lowered his head and only after a moment raised his eyes and smiled.

"How observant!" he said lightly. "Now I'm going to get dressed."

And he left the kitchen, slamming the door, as always, loudly behind him. In a moment his loud whistling could be heard from the Maleckis' bedroom where he had taken his things.

Jan stood there for a moment without moving, thoughtfully biting his lip. Finally he turned to his wife.

"My brother's really something, isn't he?"

Anna began arranging the bread she had cut on a plate.

"You know I like Julek very much."

"You barely know him!" he said, shrugging his shoulders. "You've hardly seen him more than a couple of times."

"I know," she replied "But I hardly know you either."

"Me?" he asked, genuinely surprised.

He went up to his wife and, taking her by the hands, looked straight into her eyes.

"What in the world do you mean by that?"

She merely smiled brightly.

"Nothing. That's just the way it is."

"You never put it that way before."

"Does saying it change anything?" she asked, glancing at him. "It's not only that I don't know you. You don't know me either."

And then she added more softly:

"Sometimes I think you don't even want to."

He did not reply. After a moment he withdrew his hands and went to the window.

A bluish dusk had settled on the neighborhood. The evening promised to be pleasant and calm. Down below, a light wind was blowing through the tops of the spruce trees. Crossing the street was Mr. Piotrowski, the young husband of the solidly built black marketeer on the ground floor. Wearing a light-colored hat pushed down over his forehead and with his sports coat flung over his shoulder, he sauntered toward the house. But then he came to a stop, adjusted his belted trousers, and turned around to look at a girl walking along the sidewalk in the opposite direction.

Anna was taking dishes out of the sideboard.

"Dear," she said, "Irena is in there all by herself."

"You're right," he reminded himself. "I'll go see her. Will supper be ready soon?"

"In fifteen minutes at the most."

He was about to leave when suddenly from out of the silence came the far-off report of gunfire. He stopped and began listening attentively.

"Listen!" Malecki motioned to his wife. "There!"

She came closer and they listened intently for a moment.

"There it is again!" Malecki heard a far-off burst of fire. "You can hear it distinctly!"

She only nodded her head.

"There it is again!"

Anna went back into the kitchen. In a moment she called out:

"Do you think anyone from our side will help them?"

Malecki shrugged.

"In this situation? How do you imagine it? In what way? Haven't enough of us died already, and still are dying?"

She shook her head.

"It's not that simple!"

He preferred to answer with a question:

"What isn't that simple?"

"That over there!" she pointed in the direction of the ghetto. "Maybe you will laugh at what I'm going to say."

"Me?"

"I don't know, maybe not . . . but . . ."

She became mixed up in what she wanted to say and fell silent. Jan went to her.

"Ania!" he whispered sincerely. She raised her eyes to him, as sad as he had ever seen them.

"We'll talk about it later tonight when we're alone, all right?" she said.

"Would you prefer that?"

"Yes."

"So we will!" he agreed. "I'll remind you."

"And now go in to Irena! Go ahead."

He hesitated.

"Go, dear," she repeated.

He left with a heavy heart and stood for a moment in the hallway. Julek was humming to himself in the bedroom. He must have gotten dressed, because he could be heard pacing about the room in his army boots. His tall silhouette was outlined behind the frosted glass doors. On the other side of the corridor, in what they called the study, it was quiet. Jan finally made up his mind to enter.

Irena stood leaning against a large drawing table near the half-open balcony doors. She had taken off her jacket, and the very delicate opal color of her blouse emphasized the darkness of her thick, luxuriant hair.

She turned around at the sound of the opening door.

"Excuse me," Malecki began, to justify himself, "but it seems my brother has arrived. I didn't know anything about it."

"Your brother?" she asked with surprise.

"You don't know him. Julek."

"Oh, yes!" she uttered, recalling something. "The one you were always worried about?"

"That one. But I've stopped worrying about him."

Irena looked again toward the balcony.

"Tell me, what direction do these windows face? I can't figure it out."

"East is over there," he replied, pointing in the direction of the Vistula.

"So let me see . . . ," she said, "that means the ghetto will be in that direction?"

"A little more to the south."

She glanced there fleetingly but then quickly returned to the previous topic.

"What's your brother up to?"

"Julek?" he answered indifferently. "I honestly don't know. I expect the same thing as most people his age."

Irena laughed openly:

"But he's just a kid!"

"Well, let's say so."

"Really, he is!" she said thoughtfully. "I'd forgotten you'd told me about him a long time back, three or more years ago."

They both fell to thinking at that moment about Smug and the times that had become so remote as to be unreal. Malecki preferred not to indulge in reminiscences, but before he was able to say anything to change the subject, Irena cut him off.

"You had no idea back then in Smug that one day I'd show up on your doorstep like this, did you?"

"No one did," he replied with distaste.

To his surprise she burst out laughing.

"Oh well, you have your own life now, don't you? The one you always wanted, right?"

"Yes, I do," he replied curtly.

"Well then! What more could anyone ask?"

He felt he had to respond.

"You say that as if in reproach."

"Me?" Irena said, acting genuinely surprised. "Whatever for? You're imagining it."

"You think so?"

"Of course!"

And she repaid him with his own words, uttered earlier on the stairs:

"Don't be so touchy."

He understood the allusion but let it pass. Irena turned away and took up a position in the doorway onto the balcony.

The smell of lilacs wafted in from the neighboring garden. A tall, gray-haired man was watering small, tidy rows of vegetables with a green watering can. Behind him toddled a two-year-old boy, plump and rosy, in a blue shirt and brown trousers. Children's clothing was hanging out to dry on a line strung between two blossoming apple trees. Along the path behind the garden a ragged, light-haired youth was driving a small flock of goats. A white kid frolicked along gaily in front of him.

"You know what?" Irena asked. "After a while all this serenity here could become rather irksome."

"Do you think it is all that serene?"

"Just look at this idyll!" she said, pointing at the neighbor's garden.

He moved closer.

"Well, isn't it?" she repeated.

Malecki knew the people living in this neighborhood by sight and voice. He knew that the father of the young boy had been arrested a few months earlier and had recently been executed in Pawiak prison, while his wife, the daughter of the gray-haired man, had been transported to a women's work camp in Ravensbrück. He remembered well that late-winter night (it had already begun to thaw), when the nearby rattle of a car had awoken both him and Anna from their first sleep. He had gotten up quickly and groped his way to the window in the dark. Julek had been spending the night with them. The car had approached the house very slowly, tiny drops of rain drizzling in the path of its dimmed headlights. Jan had been sure that the car would stop, and it actually had stopped right in front of their house. However, nobody got out. Then it had been quiet for a while, with only the rain whipping against the windowpanes. After a while the car had moved on and stopped a bit farther on, in front of the house next door. The headlights had turned off, so that one could not make out the people as they got out. Only the slamming of doors could be heard, while the glare of flashlights cut through the darkness. Then had come a loud banging against a door. A light had turned on in one of the windows on the bottom floor. That light had remained on practically until morning, long after the car's departure.

He wanted to tell all of this to Irena and to explain to her what really went on behind that idyll, as she called it, but the words stuck in his throat.

"Tell me," she repeated, "doesn't this look like an idyll out of a picture book, this garden, the serenity, the old man watering his rows of vegetables . . ."

"Oh, yes," he agreed. "It really does look like that."

Over supper the conversation at first touched on general matters and insignificant topics. They spoke a little about the news from the various fronts, a little about the weather, about rumors and stories circulating around Warsaw, but mostly about nothing. Julek took practically no part in the conversation. He spoke up only a couple of times and otherwise sat silent, eating hungrily and refilling his plate several times. Every once in a while he would furrow his brow with evident impatience and lower his dark, thickly arched eyebrows.

Jan did most of the talking, possibly showing even too much vivacity. At a one point, amid efforts completely out of proportion to the vapidity of the conversation, he suddenly recalled the last unsuccessful dinner in Zalesinek, when Irena had attempted to conceal her own inner distress in similar fashion. His enthusiasm immediately died, and he became lost in the middle of telling a not especially pertinent story. The conversation, which had become artificial and burdensome for all, slowly began to die down until at last it came to a complete halt in an uneasy silence. Anna, who always felt best in an atmosphere of intimate talk about essential matters, was not a skilled enough hostess to steer the mood at the dinner table in the right direction. Irena would have been able to do so had she wanted, but now she didn't feel like it.

The windows in the dining room were wide open, and the grayish-blue dusk seemed to begin in the room itself. Because of the blackout, no lights were turned on, and the semidarkness, slightly obscuring the faces of those seated at the table, made the drawn-out silence easier to bear.

Down below, in one of the apartments where the windows must also have been open, an accordion began to play. Irena lifted her head.

"That's the man on the ground floor," Jan muttered. "Piotrowski."

The sound of the accordion came closer, then moved away. Evidently Piotrowski was walking about the apartment as he played.

At that moment, the teakettle began to whistle, and Anna got up to make tea. Jan pushed some cigarettes toward Irena and then to his brother, who declined.

"I prefer my own. They're stronger!"

He took a pack of tobacco and papers out of the pocket of his sports coat and skillfully began to roll a cigarette between his fingers. As Jan unsuccessfully attempted to coax a flame out of his lighter, Julek passed the box to Irena.

"Why don't you try one of these? It's good Miechów tobacco."

With only slightly less skill than Julek, Irena began rolling one for herself.

"So you've been around Miechów lately?" she asked with evident interest.

"Among other places," he answered evasively. "Do you know those parts?"

She merely nodded.

"Where, exactly?" she asked.

"Everywhere a little."

"How about around Obarów?"

"Sure."

"It seems you've been living somewhere around there lately, right?" put in Jan.

"Yes, but not lately."

Despite the twilight penetrating more and more deeply from the outside to within the walls, it was apparent that an ironic smirk played upon her face as she bent over the table.

"Good people saw to it that I didn't stay in one place too long."

Anna set out teacups and sat down in her place between her husband and Julek. Around the table silence prevailed. Piotrowski, now probably standing right in the window, was playing some prewar song. Jan unnecessarily felt personally hurt by Irena's words. Putting out his unfinished cigarette, he said:

"I gather you have had occasion to meet not only good people?"

"No, not only good ones," she said calmly. "But do you really think that good people excuse the others?"

Before he could answer, Julek leaned over the table.

"You know what I was just thinking of, Janek? The old days when we lived together on Poznańska Street. Remember? You were going to the polytechnic institute, and I was still a schoolboy. Your friends were always dropping by—what was your club called again? Arconia,[4] right? I remember how once in the hall I counted five student caps and as many cudgels. I was so impressed! I only later found out that club members went around with their sticks to beat up Jews and smash the windows of stores on Nalewki Street . . ."

Irena observed Julek very carefully as he spoke.

"They also beat up their Jewish classmates!" she tossed in quietly.

Malecki shoved away his teacup much too violently.

"It seems to me that I neither went around with a stick nor ever approved of any such methods . . ."

Julek smiled contrarily.

"And which methods did you approve of?"

"What do you mean which ones?"

"Methods of anti-Semitism, fascism, or whatever you want to call it?"

"Me?" Jan was outraged.

Julek's unexpected words startled even Irena.

"I feel I must stand up for your brother . . ."

"Oh, please!" Jan interrupted her abruptly.

Julek energetically pushed his fair and still not completely dry hair off his brow.

"Wait. You don't understand what I'm saying. I'm not accusing him of anything," he said, indicating his brother. "But what does he mean by 'not approving of their methods'? We hear that sort of thing all the time from so-called decent Poles when they condemn crimes and violence toward the Jews. But what do these people mean? Are they really enemies of anti-Semitism? Of course not! According to them the cause is legitimate, it's just that the methods aren't. Aren't I right? I'm talking about essentials here. I know perfectly well what it means to suit one's anti-Semitism to one's tastes. We merely find the so-called methods distasteful! The point is that there shouldn't be any methods in the first place, or it's always going to end in something like that!" he concluded, pointing behind him in the direction of the distant ghetto.

Piotrowski's sentimental tango had wandered off into the distance for a moment, but now it could be heard again quite distinctly.

Anna continued sitting with her head bent over her teacup. Irena also remained silent.

Jan mechanically reached for another cigarette.

"You say the cause itself is wrong," he said, turning to his brother. "Let's have done with these mutual frictions and resentments, and so on. Fine! But does it depend only on us?"

Julek shook his head.

"I don't like empty phrases."

"They're not empty."

"Well what are they, then? They're meaningless! What good does it do if I say it depends on both us and the Jews? What am I supposed to appeal to? Mutual goodwill? It's all words, nothing but words, when words are not what is needed . . ."

Jan sank deeper into his chair.

"Well then, what *is* needed?"

Julek remained silent. Just then a sharp ring came at the door. Irena started.

"That must be Włodek!" Anna said.

Jan went to open the door, and indeed it was young Karski. As soon as Julek heard his voice, he got up from the table.

"You can use our room," Anna suggested. "You'll be able to talk in private there."

"Fifteen minutes, no more," Julek promised.

He encountered Jan in the doorway.

"You didn't answer me," Jan reminded him.

Julek laughed out loud.

"Don't worry. You'll get your answer."

Since supper was over, Anna proposed going into the study. Irena was brought back to the present by the sound of Anna's voice, and she got up heavily, looking very tired.

"Maybe you would like to lie down?" Anna asked.

She hastily declined and went with Jan into the study, while Anna stayed in the dining room to clear the table.

Dusk had settled into night, but the sky, which arched over the darkness, was still fresh and delicate, as it is only in springtime. Jan closed up the balcony, drew the blinds, and turned on a small lamp standing on a low table next to the wall. The room became very quiet.

Irena sank into an easy chair.

"Tell me," she spoke up suddenly. "What exactly am I to do? What am I supposed to do with myself?"

Jan came to a halt in the middle of the room.

"We'll think of something," he said vaguely.

"Yes, but what?"

As he frequently did, he answered her question with another one: "What exactly were you doing there on Nowiniarska Street when I ran into you?

"There? Nothing. I had just gone . . . to see what was happening."

"How could you? You were running the risk of who knows what happening . . ."

"I didn't even think about it!" she said, shrugging. "In any case, what could have happened to me? Nothing worse than what was happening to the people behind the walls."

"You said you wanted to live."

"Yes, I do," she affirmed, "but . . ."

"But what?"

"Sometimes I just can't. I really just can't."

A period of silence ensued. Piotrowski was still playing his accordion.

"Where have you been living lately?" Jan asked.

"Lately? In the Mokotów district, at the Makowskis' . . . You remember him, don't you?"

Makowski had been Professor Lilien's assistant. When the Liliens were living under the name of Grabowski and suddenly had to leave their apartment along the Otwock line, the professor, after returning from Kraków, had stayed with him for a couple of weeks. Malecki knew the young historian from better days in Smug.

"And then what?" He sat down in the armchair opposite her. "Something happened?"

She nodded her head.

"What?"

"What always happens!" she answered curtly.

She had lived with the Makowskis for a few weeks. Since she hardly left the house at all, she had thought she was safe. Someone, however, must have found out about her presence. Just that morning, unbeknownst to the Makowskis, two young men had turned up at the house, one of them a Gestapo agent. Despite her Aryan documents, they had taken her to a car waiting in front of the building. They had been very polite but did not hide the fact that they were driving her to Gestapo headquarters on Szuch Avenue. Along the way she had ransomed herself with her last gold five-ruble coin. She had gotten out near Szuch, but was afraid to return to Mokotów.

"So the Makowskis don't know anything about it?" he asked.

"No!"

Jan said he would undertake to go to them next day, tell them everything, and bring Irena some of her belongings.

"It obviously doesn't make sense for you to return there now!" he decided. "Best not to take a chance."

She rather indifferently agreed that he was probably right.

"But what now?" she lowered her head. "What now? How am I supposed to go on? I'll never be able to live like a normal person. Do you know that whenever I meet someone new, I automatically look into their eyes and ask myself whether they would be capable of turning me in? It's terrible . . . you have no idea how terrible it is . . ."

At that moment Anna entered the study. She paused for a moment in the door and then quietly sat down on the daybed.

Irena raised her head and looked at Jan.

"Do you know that when I met you today, I had exactly the same thought?"

He did not reply.

"If I can only make it through to the end."

"Then everything will be different," he put in.

"No, people don't change," she contradicted him. "But at least then they won't have the legal right to kill me. You'll see that people like those two young men who took me away today in their car will look at me contemptuously and regret only that they can't extort another stupid five rubles from me."

"Don't talk nonsense!" he blurted out.

"You'll see! We'll be even more despised then than now, because we'll be free to walk down the street. We'll return to our apartments and our occupations and we'll regain our rights. Don't tell me I'm wrong—I know how it will be, and so do you. At present a simple sense of shame prevents many people from showing open hostility toward us. They shelter us out of compulsion and hide us out of a sense of obligation. But then there will be no one to force them to. And we for our part will never forget anything, for you know that Jews never forget a wrong. Completely different from you people. You forget about everything, both when you have been wronged and when you have done wrong."

He couldn't contradict her, for he felt the same way she did. As for him, in the depths of his heart and mind he needed and desired nothing more than to forget about everything. He would have liked at least to defend his national weakness, to justify and ennoble it somehow.

"Isn't that just what hope is?" he mused.

"What?" She did not understand.

"Forgetfulness!"

And he pursued it further:

"The hope that things will get better. Are we supposed to drag these nightmarish years with us through the rest of our lives, never to break with them?"

"I don't know," she said. "But during the past year I've become someone completely different from the person I used to be. I have been forced to become different. That much has already been accomplished, it seems, so how can I forget about it?"

"These years have changed everyone," Jan assented.

"But not everyone has had his dignity taken away!"

Anna, who for the entire time had been sitting cross-legged without moving on the edge of the daybed, suddenly lifted her head.

"Can one really take away someone's dignity?" she asked quietly.

Irena turned to her.

"Can one? Oh, yes! Believe me one can. One can tear anything out of people: their freedom, self-respect, desire, hope, everything! Even their fear . . . I have seen it with my own eyes, I have witnessed it personally . . . Do you know how my father died?"

It was during the time when the Germans had begun their first collective murder of the Jews, the summer of 1942. The professor had been staying at the time with Irena on an estate in the Miechów district. Mrs. Lilien had lived for a while on the outskirts of Kraków but soon had to go into the country as well. The presence of the Liliens had been rather well disguised. Irena was an office worker in a distillery, while the professor remained on the manor in the capacity of a tutor for the owner's sons. They had floated through the first few months of their visit peacefully, and it seemed that at last, after so many hardships, they would be able live again and to survive. All that had remained was to bring Irena's mother there. But just when her arrival had finally been arranged, the anti-Jewish repressions began, and before long they had reached the neighborhood in which Irena and her father were hiding. One day toward nightfall in Obarów, the closest town, a special punitive detachment of Gestapo officers had arrived and begun to murder the Jews. The owner of the estate had received an anonymous phone call, from which it emerged that the Germans knew all about the Liliens and their origins. There had been no choice but to flee.

Hiding the Liliens on any of the nearby estates was impossible, and a departure for Kraków, considering the danger along the roads, was also out of the question for the moment. Besides that, the professor had been feeling very poorly, not having entirely recovered from a recent serious bout of influenza. He had always had a weak heart. Given the circumstances, shelter in the neighboring forest had seemed to represent the only possibility of escape. The Liliens' landlord had so advised them, and the professor and Irena agreed. They were to take shelter in a forester's cabin about eight kilometers from the estate and wait out the most dangerous period. The professor had not wanted any of the servants or estate workers to escort them, for he no longer had faith in people and trusted almost no one, so they had gone alone . . .

The entry door slammed in the living room, and Irena broke off her story. After a moment, Julek appeared in the study. Surveying the gathering, he discerned that he had interrupted some kind of conversation and moved to one side. Taking out some tobacco, he began to roll himself a cigarette.

"And then what?" asked Jan.

"It was a terrible night!" she began again. "It was pitch black, and we didn't know the neighborhood very well. At first we were somewhat familiar with the woods, but when we had to get off the road and go along the paths we got completely lost. It was only later, when it started to get light, that I discovered that we had gone in the wrong direction. Father was barely able to walk, and we continually had to stop and rest. His heart was very weak. He had become a completely different person. He looked like a sick old Jew, a cowering little Jew afraid to die. He was terribly afraid of falling into the hands of the Germans. We would sit and rest for a little, and then he would suddenly jump up. It still seemed to him that the lodge must be somewhere close by. I already knew we wouldn't reach it, but he was still under the delusion that we would.

"When dawn arrived, we came onto some road. It wasn't completely light yet, but still gray . . . Father didn't want to go out onto the road, so I went myself, and then I saw it, a large, dark column moving toward us. Can you imagine what I felt then? I wanted to run at once into the thick of the woods, but father couldn't go on. He had gone awfully pale and begun to shake. I thought it was the end. So we hid in some bushes by side of the road, down below, where it was thick—alders, I think. We lay on the ground. Father was breathing heavily and constantly shivering as if from the cold. It took a dreadfully long time for those people to reach us. I pressed my face to the ground. Dew covered the grass, and if I had lain there any longer, I would probably have fallen asleep. I was that tired. Then suddenly I heard my father's voice, completely changed and quavering: 'Irena! Those are Jews!' I lifted my head and saw that the crowd was now not far off and that they really were Jews, all of them. Women, old folk, and children, the poorest of the Jewish poor. I later found out that they were the Jews of Obarów, the ones the Nazis hadn't had time to shoot during the night. They were being driven along to some collection point along with Jews from other towns and villages from all over the district. You have no idea what a sight it was. I'll never forget it. People all herded together, pressed up against one another, some of them barefoot, carrying bundles, all of them dirty and covered with dust, with pale and pain-worn faces, some of them bloody. Women were carrying little children in their arms. One little girl, dark-haired and thin, wearing a pink percale polka-dot dress, was carrying two babies, one in her arms and the other on her back.

"At first I didn't even notice anyone guarding them, but after a minute I saw a German soldier walking alongside them on the grass, probably so as not to get dust on his shiny boots. He looked so young and innocent. He was just a boy, maybe seventeen or eighteen years old. He passed right by me, a couple of steps away, so close I could hear his boots squeak.

"Suddenly I sensed my father get up off the ground. I remember that I wanted to shout and hold him back, but no. It's hard to describe what I was

going through then. I knew I ought to do something and not let him leave, to
go after him, but I did nothing but lie there motionless and watch. I saw my
father stand up on the edge of the road, hunched and bent over. As soon as
they saw him, several people walking nearest to him came to a stop. I could
see their eyes, their vacant stares, almost as if blind. They stopped and looked
at my father with uncomprehending eyes. Then that young soldier turned
around and, probably thinking that father had gotten out of line, shouted and
ran up to him, struck him several times in the head with his riding crop, and
shoved him so violently he fell down. Then he ran up to him again and kicked
him several times. An old woman tried to help my father get up, but she also
got it with the whip, and my father finally managed to get up on his own, first
on all fours and then standing. I remember closing my eyes and when I
opened them, I could no longer find my father among the crowd. They all
looked the same."

No one said anything for some time.

"Maybe they weren't killed," said Jan. "Couldn't they have been sent to
work camps?"

"What are you saying?" said Julek, moving from his place next to the
wall. "Don't you know what those things look like? They set up a so-called
collection point along the highway and they drive Jews from the entire area
into it. Then they make a selection and take away the young, the healthy, and
the strong to work camps. The rest are killed on the spot. Like the ones walking up that road . . . the children, the women, the old . . ."

"Yes," confirmed Irena. "They are ordered to dig pits, and then the machine guns are set up."

Julek moved closer. In the semidarkness, with his tall boots and military-
cut breeches, he seemed larger than he really was.

"Do you know who asked me about you recently? He thought I must
know you."

She looked at him inquisitively.

"Stefan Weinert."

The Weinerts were close relatives of Mrs. Lilien, and Stefan was of Irena's
age.

"You don't say!" Irena said brightly. "I didn't know Stefan was alive."

"Yes, he is."

"Where did you see him? His parents were murdered."

"I know. Stefan was also imprisoned, but that's another story. The guy got lucky and managed to escape."

"Where is he now?"

Julek smiled.

"Beyond the Bug.[5] In the forest."

Irena fell to thinking.

"Tell him hello from me. You'll see him again, won't you?"

"Who knows?" said Julek, pushing his hair off his forehead. "Maybe."

At that moment a series of shots rang out from the yard, quickly, one after the other. Irena instinctively started. The shots had not yet died down when they were joined by the rattle of an automatic pistol. Now Anna, too, arose from the daybed.

"Here we go again!" muttered Julek.

Irena paled.

"Better turn out the light," she whispered.

Jan quickly flicked the switch, and the room was plunged into darkness.

The shots came closer, their echoes reverberating among the quiet, narrow streets.

"They're coming straight toward us!" Julek noted out loud.

"Shhh!" Jan hissed, so loud did his brother's voice seem. Julek, in the meantime, went to the window and began to roll up the blind.

"Are you crazy?" Jan protested.

But the night was already open before them. Julek lightly pushed ajar the door to the balcony and stood there. Anna and Jan moved forward automatically, leaving only Irena in the middle of the room. The chill air, saturated with the smell of springtime earth, began to enter the apartment. A starlit sky shone overhead.

"I can't see anything," Julek whispered.

The shooting stopped, leaving a vast silence in its wake. Suddenly Julek motioned sharply to his brother and sister-in-law standing behind him, and they moved closer.

Despite the dark, one could make out the shadow of a man running quickly down the sidewalk.

Suddenly an automatic pistol began to fire, this time from very close by. Anna instinctively grasped her husband's hand. He embraced her tightly and held her close.

The man stopped, bent down, and knelt under the protection of the nearest tree, a young and very frail acacia. From his hiding place, he began to fire into the darkness of the empty street. It lasted barely a second, for he abruptly broke off and began to run further, still bent over. Shots rang out all around him.

Julek withdrew into the room. The heavy tramp of soldiers' hobnailed boots could clearly be heard. A moment later, the loud, guttural shouts of the Germans resounded in the darkness. There were several of them, some running in the middle of the street, others along the sidewalk.

Malecki tugged at his brother's arm. Suddenly one of the running soldiers stopped near a fence enclosing the lot and called out sharply to one of his comrades. One could clearly make out his tall, strongly outlined and somewhat stooped figure, with low-set helmet and automatic pistol at the ready. A few others stopped as well. He started to say something to them, pointing in the direction of the Maleckis' house.

"It's all over now!" Jan thought. Immediately beyond their villa, the last one in the development, stretched an empty field. The soldiers in all likelihood had concluded that the fugitive, taking advantage of the darkness, had hidden in one of the neighboring houses or gardens. In the event of an inspection, the discovery in the same apartment of two unregistered people, one of them a young man with a weapon and the other a Semitic-looking woman, would be enough for them to line everyone up against a wall and shoot them.

Irena, who from inside the room could not see anything but who could still sense the tension, stirred.

"What is happening out there?" she asked in a low, hoarse voice.

Julek quickly withdrew from the doorway, pulling Jan and Anna after him.

"Get into the dining room!" he said in a calm, even whisper. "In the bedroom in my suitcase there's a package . . . small, wrapped in paper . . . hide it, Anna!"

She nodded.

"And above all, stay calm! Everything will be all right . . ."

Irena wanted to say something, but he shoved her toward the door.

"Quick, get out of here! I'll come to you if I need to."

When they had left, he returned to the window. Three soldiers stood in the same spot deliberating among themselves. The rest had evidently run on toward the field.

Julek knew that everything, or at least very much, might now depend on his calm self-assuredness. He had found himself in similar situations on more than one occasion, and his mind worked smoothly and efficiently. However, he did not feel in himself the same equanimity and self-mastery he strove for and usually achieved in such situations. He continued to stare intently ahead at the silhouettes of the hated enemy soldiers outlined against the night at about a gunshot's distance. He knew that every move of those people ought to intensify his vigilance and stifle in him any rash impulses. At the same time, he could not get away from the thought of what might happen to his brother and Anna in case the matter took a more serious turn. When he imagined that Anna would surely be able to remain calm to the very end and when he thought of what would become of her, he was overtaken by a wave of fear stronger than any he had ever experienced before.

One of the soldiers separated from his comrades and began to walk toward the gate. The other two soon followed. Julek lost sight of them but then heard the squeaking of the gate and their heavy, even tread in front of the house. For a moment his heart stopped beating. He clenched his fists, shut his eyes, and instantly the terrible tension he had felt vanished. His calm returned. He had just reached for his revolver in order to hide it between the balcony doors when, from beyond the houses, in the direction of the fields, the sharp sounds of automatic pistol fire rang out and echoed among the buildings.

The soldiers downstairs came to a halt and began talking. After a moment, they hurriedly turned back, and it became quiet. Then more shots rang out, but this time much farther away, somewhere in the distant reaches of the night.

Julek replaced his pistol in his trousers and brushed back his hair. "Whew," he thought to himself.

He crossed back into the hall and opened the door to the dining room. The lights were turned low, but the scene was clearly visible. Jan was sitting at the table reading a book, while next to him Anna was playing solitaire. Only Irena was making no pretense of being busy. Her face was pale, constricted, and sunken, and her hands trembled uncontrollably. It would not have required great observational skill at that moment to have taken her for a Jew.

Seeing Julek, Jan put aside his book and got up.

"Have they gone?"

Julek waved his hand contemptuously.

"I hope that guy doesn't get caught! But they won't be back; we can sleep in peace."

Automatic fire again rattled out from somewhere very far away, by now more sporadic, as if done for show.

Julek leaned against the table and over toward Anna, who with steady movements was still playing solitaire.

"Well?" he asked softly. "Are you winning?"

Anna lifted her head and softly laid down her cards.

"Unfortunately not," she smiled. "I can't win, because I made a mistake in the deal."

Julek said nothing in reply.

"Well," Jan spoke up, "I can't say it has been the most pleasant of evenings."

Then Irena got up.

"Listen! I hear voices again . . ."

They listened intently for a minute or so to the total quiet.

"There's nothing to hear," Julek said. "I'm sure of it. I have a good ear."

But Irena, unconvinced, went into the study, and after a moment her muffled cry could be heard.

She stood in the center of the room, her face turned toward the balcony.

"Look!" she whispered in a dry, hoarse voice. "See how bright it is . . ."

A huge, pinkish glow reached high up into the sky, illuminating the distant dark of night.

"It's burning!" Julek said.

The fire was becoming wider and wider and more bloody looking, encompassing the heart of the night with its glow.

The Maleckis did not fall asleep for a long time. Julek barely undressed at all, but noisily tossed his boots onto the floor. He must have fallen asleep right away, because when Jan shortly thereafter returned from the bathroom, the dining room was dark and silent. No light burned in the study either, though muffled, circling steps came from inside the room.

Anna was already in bed. Jan sat next to her and laid his hand on hers.

"Are you tired?"

She was tired.

"What a horrible day!" he exclaimed. " A little too much all at once . . ."

The glow of the lamp glared in Anna's eyes, so he pushed the light aside and leaned over her.

"You had something to tell me, remember?"

She simply nodded.

"What was it?"

"Different things . . ."

"You don't want to tell me what?"

She rose slightly and leaned on her arm.

"I'd rather not," she honestly admitted and quickly explained: "It's no secret, dear, but it's just hard to talk about it . . ."

"About what?"

"About that!" Her eyes glanced toward the window.

He guessed that she meant the uprising in the ghetto.

"I know," he agreed.

"You see, I'm at a loss for words when I think about those people over there and what awaits them. And what they must think about us . . . here on this side."

"More of us are dying than they are."

"Yes," she replied, "but it's not the same thing."

She wanted to add how important and essential to her was the faith in which she had been raised and in which she still believed, finding in it confirmation of the eternal sense and order of the world; and how for her, as a believing Catholic, the tragedy of the Jews, having already festered for so many centuries, was the most painful test of all for a Christian conscience. Who, if not Christians, ought to be moved by the cruel fate of that least fortunate of all peoples, a tribe that, having once rejected the truth, now bore the weight of that betrayal through unimaginable sufferings, humiliations, and wrongs? Who, if not a Christian, ought to do everything in his power to lighten the misfortune of these downtrodden people and to be with them, as they died alone and without hope? However, as much as she thought about such matters, she could not now summon up the strength to talk about them.

Jan did not insist, but got into bed and turned out the light.

"You know," she said after a while in the dark, "by next Easter our child will already be big, he'll be starting to walk."

He allowed himself to be carried along by her thoughts, in order to free himself from his own.

"Yes, by next summer he'll be starting to walk."

"Next summer!" she repeated. "When one puts it that way, it seems so simple, so ordinary, doesn't it?"

"A year from now!"

"Yes, but when one tries to think what things will look like in a year, it's like looking into a complete void. Can you imagine that our child might ever have to live through such terrible times as these?"

Jan placed his hands behind his head and looked into the darkness overhead.

"Our parents didn't imagine it either."

"Don't talk that way," she whispered reproachfully. "Not so long ago, I still thought that the world would never change. But now I can't think that way anymore. I still have to believe that our child will grow up in different and better times."

Neither said anything for a long time.

"Are you asleep?" she asked.

"No," he replied in a completely sober voice.

"It's probably still burning."

He sat up in bed.

"I'll go and see."

He cast off the quilt, walked barefoot to the window, and raised the blind.

The glare was immense, even larger than before, and its bloody reflection illuminated the entire southern portion of the sky.

Jan opened the window and leaned out. The night was chilly but still smelled of spring. From very far off, measured pulses of cannon fire could be heard. The night trembled without cease.

"Can you hear it?"

"Yes!" she whispered.

The longer he listened, the more terrifying and threatening the relentless thundering of the burning night seemed to be. Then he shuddered. A strange, piercing noise unlike any he had ever heard before in his life sounded in the distance.

Anna got out of bed and knelt on the bedspread.

"What was that?"

Jan instinctively withdrew from the window.

"I don't know. How can it be possible?"

"Shut the window!" Anna begged. "I can't listen to it."

Before he could close it, Irena, obviously just awakened from her first sleep, ran out of the study into the corridor.

Jan quickly opened the door to the hall and flicked the switch. She stood next to the door to the bathroom, dressed only in her nightshirt, hunched and trembling, with her hands over her ears.

"Did you hear that?" she looked at him with a vacant stare. "What is it? Who is screaming like that? Can those be human voices?"

Chapter 3 ⅠⅠⅠ

BY THE NEXT DAY the fires had spread. At first it was difficult to determine who had set fire to the houses: the Germans or the Jews withdrawing from the walls into the heart of the ghetto. Later it turned out to have been the Germans.

Among the first buildings to burn from the night of the twentieth to the twenty-first were the large apartment houses along Bonifraterska Street that the Jews had defended for such a long time. The neighboring buildings caught fire from them, and when Malecki went to his office as usual at eight o'clock, an immense cloud of black smoke could be seen from afar, rising over the ghetto and covering the sky overhead. The day was sunny, but breezy, and the wind coming from that direction carried with it the acrid stench of burning to as far away as Żoliborz.

The fighting by now had shifted from Bonifraterska to Stawki Street in the Muranów district, and it must have been quite heated, because from around the Żoliborz viaduct, which was as far as the streetcars ran, everything shook from the ceaseless volleys. Apparently, in the early morning a group of insurrectionists had succeeded in getting out beyond the ghetto walls and had taken the battle as far as the forts of the Citadel. Now it was quiet in that district, and well-fortified posts guarded the exits from all the tiny streets leading from the ghetto.

In the meantime, whipped by the winds, fires burned uncontrollably all along Bonifraterska. Although the day was sunny, the sky overhead had become gray-blue and translucent, as if glazed over. People walked through this netherworld like ghosts. The crowds hurrying from Żoliborz, Marymont, and Bielany exited the streetcars in silence and in silence hastened to board flatbed trucks to transport them to the center of town. The trucks departed one after the other, shattering the silence with the din of their motors.

Farther down along Bonifraterska, now completely dead and deserted, the air had become even darker. From the windows of one of the far-off houses, sharp red tongues of fire writhed out of a massive cloud of black smoke.

It was the Wednesday before Easter.

|||

Malecki first had to take care of company business forgotten amid the previous day's confusion, after which he remained quite busy for the rest of the day, only returning home shortly before curfew. With all these matters to attend to, there had been no opportunity to go to the Makowskis in Mokotów.

As dusk settled, the fires looked even more sinister than they had that morning. Buildings were now burning quite close to the place where the streetcars stopped.

As Malecki stepped down from a horse-drawn platform wagon, he saw that the roof of the corner building at the intersection of Bonifraterska and Muranowska streets was on fire. The building was five stories high, and the fire billowed and seethed high above the ground, turning everything dark with its thick smoke. The wind swept sparks onto the roofs of the houses closest to the walls, and a fire brigade was standing next to one of the houses most in danger. Tiny black silhouettes of people scurried over the roof amid the smoke and blaze.

The battle still raged in Muranów. Machine guns and automatic rifles rattled, as time and again the earth was shaken by powerful detonations.

The fires had been visible from Bielany throughout the day. While they did not look as ominous as at night, the clouds of smoke rising into the clear blue sky still served as a constant reminder of what was going on in town. Sounds of explosions could be heard there as well.

Whether she was pretending or whether she had in fact overcome her attack of nerves, Irena behaved quite calmly compared to the preceding day. Anna had to take care of various household chores, and she was so successful in engaging Irena in everyday trifles that at times she seemed to forget entirely about her immediate troubles.

Anna's outward calm, however, was maintained through considerable effort. Although there was no reason for her to be more concerned about her husband on this particular day than on any other, she continued to fret about his being away from home all day.

Julek arose very early, before six o'clock, and this time got dressed very quietly and without slamming any doors. He seemingly would have left without even eating breakfast had Anna, who herself had just awakened, not arisen and intercepted him in the hallway.

The entire house was still asleep. It was quiet all around, the day outside barely turning gray.

"Wait!" she whispered. "You have to eat something."

He blustered that it was not necessary, but nevertheless obediently went into the kitchen, dressed in his coat and cap.

"Take off your things!" she admonished him. "I'll put on some coffee."

"But I really don't have time," he started to explain. "It doesn't make sense. I have to get going!"

He spoke in such a persuasive tone that she hesitated.

"Are you sure? It won't take long . . . fifteen minutes at most . . . In a quarter of an hour you'll be on your way!"

He felt she would be upset if he left without having breakfast.

"Well, all right!" he decided.

Anna brightened up.

"That's better!"

She lit the stove and put on water for coffee, covered the table with a tablecloth, and began taking out bread, butter, and white cheese from the sideboard. Julek, still in his cap and coat, looked on in silence. Anna noticed.

"Why do you still have your things on? Take off your coat, for heaven's sake!"

"All right," murmured Julek, as if roused from meditation.

He sat down at the table and continued looking at Anna as she stood at the stove waiting for the water to boil.

"You know," he said suddenly, "family life is not all that bad an idea."

She turned to him.

"You don't mean to say you've only just noticed?"

"Actually, yes," he openly admitted. "You know Jan and I grew up without a real home."

Their parents, who had settled in the provinces around Lublin, both had died when the boys were still young. Jan had just been finishing high school, and Julek had been barely ten years old. From that time on they had lived together in rented rooms, assisted from time to time by small infusions of cash from their father's brother, an accountant in a large sugar-beet concern in Po-merania. By the age of sixteen Julek was already independent and living alone.

"So, get married!" Anna said seriously.

Julek laughed out loud.

"After the war!"

Then he added softly:

"But of course only if I meet someone like you."

Anna blushed and leaned closer to the water beginning to boil.

"I see you're starting to pay me compliments."

"I mean it," he said in a different, more earnest tone.

As Anna had promised, breakfast was over in fifteen minutes.

"When will you be back?" she asked, when he had arisen from the table. Julek was pulling on his coat.

"I don't know," he replied slowly. "I don't know yet. I have certain plans, but I don't know what will become of them . . ."

And so it was that Anna spent the entire day alone with Irena, except for when Mrs. Karski, the major's wife, dropped by in the afternoon for a visit.

Mrs. Karski, who usually repeated uncritically all the rumors circulating about town, this time brought news—from what she claimed was a very reliable source—concerning an imminent uprising. By her account, it was to break out at any moment. She then related in detail the latest political assassinations, which, in fact, were occurring quite frequently at that time. No day passed without several German officials, policemen, or Gestapo officers being killed. The major's wife embellished the facts, of course, and asserted that everything happening in the ghetto was merely the beginning of the end and a prelude to momentous events yet to come.

She was very excited and spoke hastily and nervously, smoking one cigarette after the other. She had also managed to acquire a good bit of information about the shots fired the previous night. It was said that a cache of ammunition had been discovered in one of the more distant villas on Ceg-łowska Street. According to another version, it was not ammunition but a clandestine press. In reality, as Anna later learned, the dimensions of the incident were not nearly so dramatic but resulted merely from the accidental apprehension by a German patrol of a couple of young men out after curfew. One of them died on the spot, while the other, it seemed, managed to escape.

When Mrs. Karski finally managed to disentangle herself from the web of the latest news, she turned to an interpretation of the various predictions continually floating about town. According to these forecasts, the present and fifth year of the war was to be the last. The major's wife seemed to draw unusually strong hope from these fragile and foggy rumors, although it may only have appeared that way. Possibly her optimism was not so firmly grounded. For on what, after all, could it be grounded? A terribly difficult lot had befallen her. Besides her husband in the prison camp, she had no other close family and had to scrape and scratch to feed her growing son Włodek and little daughter Tereska in addition to sending food packages to the camp. She always had a myriad of tasks on her hands and innumerable deals and transactions of the most varied kinds imaginable, most of them leading to nothing.

So it was that now, although she complained of a slightly elevated temperature (her lungs of late had been giving her trouble), she was hastening to town, for one of her acquaintances had called to tell her that there was an opportunity to buy—at a bargain price—five hundred pairs of men's shoes. She hoped to find a purchaser for them and, although she had no one specific in mind, she had already begun to calculate the profit and even to make plans for spending the money on her most urgent household needs. Unfortunately, even if the profit were substantial, these needs were far too many and too great, and just thinking about them frightened her.

"My strength simply fails me," she said finally, calming down. "I have no idea what I'll do if I can't sell those shoes . . ."

Her greatest worry, however, and the cause of unending concern and distress, was Włodek. Although he was quite attached to his mother, she felt that over the past year he had increasingly slipped out from under her vigilance and care. She was no longer able to keep track of where he spent so much time away from home, when he would be home, or who his friends were. He deflected her questions with evasive answers and generalities, causing her terrible distress and leading her to think the worst. For days on end and at night when fear woke her from sleep, she was tortured by the thought that Włodek would commit some act of foolishness and recklessly let himself be drawn into matters too serious and onerous for a boy of sixteen.

She was unable to reconcile herself to the fact that he had ceased to be a child. Włodek was her greatest love, hope, and pride. At the same time, from various things he said, from his passing glances and silences, and even from his heartfelt smiles and caresses, she could discern some danger threatening the boy. Still, she dared not step forward and openly intervene in his secret and unknown life.

On more than one occasion she had wanted to have a heart-to-heart talk with Włodek, but she was afraid of what he might say. She foresaw what his arguments would be, and she felt that she could not stand up to them, for they were based on the same life truths she had instilled in him since childhood.

She had given all of this considerable thought before deciding to go downstairs to see the Maleckis with the intention of finding out about the particulars of Włodek's conversation with Julek yesterday. She had not met Julek herself but had only heard about him from Włodek, who had mentioned him several times of late in connection with youth meetings that had been taking place with some frequency and that, according to Włodek, were aimed at self-education. Although Włodek mentioned Julek Malecki only indifferently and in passing, she had learned enough to read her son's thoughts and knew that beneath his outwardly cool and even ironic stance toward Julek, there lay the most ardent admiration and fervent allegiance.

In the end, she did not speak with Anna about the one thing that concerned her the most, and she left without bringing it up.

||||

In view of high wartime prices and the additional expenses connected with an expected increase in family size, the Maleckis were not planning to celebrate the Easter holiday this year. Anna, however, had decided to surprise her husband by secretly baking for him an inexpensive Easter cake. The idea greatly appealed to Irena, and she immediately began to recall various fancy cake recipes from their home in Smug. Unfortunately, all were too expensive or, because of present limitations, impossible to carry out. Finally, after long deliberation, the most sensible recipe turned out to be Mrs. Karski's, already devised for wartime. Irena regretted that nothing remained of the Liliens' masterpieces, but she became thoroughly wrapped up in the Easter-cake business and eagerly helped Anna to make it. Since dinner was planned for that evening after Jan's return from work, Anna fixed a brunch, and these activities occupied her and Irena the entire morning. After brunch, Anna needed to leave the house to make various purchases.

The day was pleasant and warm, full of sunshine, except that the sky, which was clear and springlike above Bielany, was darkened by the fires over town. But the fight was taking place far away. People considered by many to be foreigners were dying behind those infamous walls, but neither their isolated defense nor the fate that awaited them changed the course of everyday life.

On the stairway of a basement-level store on Banasiak Street, Anna ran into stout Mrs. Piotrowski climbing up the stairs with a large bag of provisions.

"Oh, hello, Mrs. Malecki, I see you're also doing some holiday shopping!" she said, coming to a stop upon seeing her.

Anna replied that she was not celebrating the holidays this year. Mrs. Piotrowski smiled understandingly.

"Of course that's what people always say, but when one has guests in the house . . ."

"Yes, my husband's brother has come to stay for several days," Anna explained too hurriedly.

Under Mrs. Piotrowski's indulgent gaze, she immediately concluded that she had erred by not freely admitting to Irena's presence, and tried to fix it.

"Besides him there's an old friend of mine, but I'm not sure whether she's staying for the holidays, probably not . . ."

Mrs. Piotrowski nodded her head as if sympathetically and took up another subject.

"You know what I just heard? Such a tragedy! In Saska Kępa they caught a Jew in one of the houses. He was hiding there, like they do, you know. And for one Jew, my dear lady, they shot five of our people. Tell me if that's not a tragedy!"

Anna remained silent for a moment.

"Yes, it is," she finally affirmed.

"So much innocent blood!" said Mrs. Piotrowski, advancing a step. "In my opinion, my dear lady, any Pole who hides a Jew in his home is, if you don't mind my saying so, nothing but a swine! I'm a Pole and that's what I say!" she said, striking her breast. "It's unchristian for good Catholics to have to die for a single solitary Jew. That simply cannot stand!"

"No, it simply cannot stand!" she repeated emphatically. "Everyone values his own life. We're not suffering through the occupation just to die needlessly for the Jews!"

Anna decided not to mention this conversation to Jan, preferring to spare him new worries. She did not actually think Mrs. Piotrowski would go so far as to denounce anyone, but even so Anna returned home with a heavy heart.

The children were playing in front of the house: Wacek Piotrowski, chubby-cheeked and strongly resembling his mother; Stefcio, the son of the Osipowiczes from the third floor, who was hopping about like a kangaroo; and Tereska Karski, sunburnt as a little Gypsy.

Mr. Piotrowski was sunning himself in the wide-open window of the ground floor. Whistling through his teeth, he sat lounging on the windowsill, his dark chest hair bristling from behind his unbuttoned shirt as he supported himself with his shoulders and bare feet against the window frame. As Anna passed, he gave her the once-over with a languid and somewhat leering gaze.

||||

While Anna was out, Irena hardly knew what to do with herself. Since the whole morning had been taken up with trivial household matters, it was only now that she found herself alone and with nothing to do that she began to feel like a prisoner. For how many months now had she struggled against and overcome the urge to move about freely? No matter where she found herself, she had to hide her presence, to take care at every step, lest it be noticed on the outside that she so much as existed. Such freedom as she had was cramped and fragile, confined within four walls. The longer she had to live under such detention, humiliatingly concealing her Semitic appearance, the more burdensome the effort became.

The doors onto the balcony had been left wide open, and the balcony itself was swathed in sunlight. From down below, somewhere beyond the house, she could hear the shouts of children playing.

The temptation to breathe the warm air suddenly overtook her so strongly that she could not stop herself from going out onto the balcony. For a moment she stood with her head tilted back, intoxicated with the springtime warmth. She felt so good that the ability to indulge herself in even such a limited freedom seemed like something close to happiness. But barely had she looked down when she saw a young man who must already have noticed her presence, for he was openly gazing up toward the balcony.

He was standing a little off to the side in an unbuttoned shirt and with his hands buried in his pants pockets. Irena shuddered, but was able to control herself and did not retreat too quickly. She even forced herself to look indifferently in that direction. She guessed right away that this must be Piotrowski. Perceiving that she was looking at him, he smiled at her roguishly.

When Anna returned, Irena was lying on the daybed with a French copy of *The Charterhouse of Parma.*[1] But she was not reading it. Resting her head on her hands, she looked out the window. The daybed was low and pushed back against the wall, so that from her half-lying position she could see only the sky. A trail of gray, murky smoke crept slowly across it, finally penetrating the cloudless azure above. The cries of children sounded from down below. The graceful chirp of little Tereska could clearly be heard against the background of the boys' noisy shouts.

"How many children there are here!" Irena observed.

Anna sat down beside her on the daybed, rather tired.

Irena continued listening.

"That little girl has such a lovely voice," she spoke up after a moment. "She chirps so sweetly . . ."

"That's Mrs. Karski's little daughter," Anna explained. "She was born during the war."

Irena regarded Anna thoughtfully.

"You surely must be glad to be having a baby?" she suddenly asked.

"Oh yes, very much!" Anna openly admitted.

"Do you already have a layette for the child? That must cost quite a bit nowadays . . ."

Anna nodded her head.

"Yes, quite a lot. But we've received things from different people, and some things I've sewn myself."

"You can sew?" Irena asked, surprised.

"Well, yes, it's not a hard thing to do . . ."

"I was never able to learn!" Irena exclaimed and added, "Please show me some of the baby things, if you would!"

As soon as they entered the Maleckis' bedroom, Irena noticed the tiny wicker bassinet standing next to the wall.

Anna had pulled out the lower drawer from a dresser filled with baby linens. Here were tiny shirts, sleepers, bibs, sweaters, blankets, towels, diapers, and the most merry, silly, and various sorts of trifles, all carefully and evenly folded and put away.

"Did you really sew all of this yourself?" asked Irena, leaning over the drawer.

"For the most part."

"There's so much of it!"

Anna smiled.

"It just seems that way . . . Those little flannel sleepers," she pointed at them, "are made out of Jan's old pajamas. And these little shirts are made from a blouse of mine . . . you see, I actually got three out of it!"

Irena greatly livened up and began to rummage through the soft flannels and cottons, lifting up the tiny blue sleepers to see them better under the light, and laughing as she saw how small they were. At one point, while examining amid the general merriment the prettiest of the little shirts, she noticed several photographs in old-fashioned beaten copper frames arranged one next to another on the dresser and she leaned toward them.

"Those are your parents, right?"

Anna nodded.

"And those three there must be your brothers?"

"Yes, my brothers."

Irena, leaning more comfortably against the dresser, continued examining the pictures.

"You take after your mother," she observed. "You have the same pretty eyes. And your brothers must be older than you, except for that one. He's younger, right?"

"Yes, he was the youngest out of the four of us, Grześ."

"Was?" Irena was taken aback.

"Yes, he's dead," Anna explained calmly. "He died in September in Modlin."[2]

"Oh, I see," said Irena in some consternation. Trying to gloss over it, she asked hastily:

"And your parents?"

"My mother's in Wilno. The Germans shot my father the moment they entered Lithuania."

She settled alongside Irena next to the dresser and examined the photographs from up close.

"Out of our entire family, only my mother and maybe my eldest brother are still alive, that one there!" Anna said, pointing at his picture, evidently taken a long time ago, for he still looked quite young. "He was in our army in England, and then we had news he was in Norway, and later in Africa. We haven't had any letters from him for quite some time. This one here, Franek, died last year in Dachau . . ."

It was quiet in the room for a moment.

"You have lost so many people close to you," whispered Irena.

"Yes," Anna nodded. "I had a very good father and wonderful brothers. We were all very close."

She straightened up and, returning to the dresser, carefully began to put away the scattered garments.

Irena silently and attentively watched Anna's heavy movements. It was difficult for her to bend over, so she knelt down on the floor.

"Here's another one!" said Irena, remembering that she still held one of the little sleepers in her hands.

Anna smiled with her brown eyes.

"That one's for the baptism. It's the prettiest!"

Irena trembled as if something was tugging at her insides.

"Haven't you ever rebelled against senseless death, at least of those closest to you?"

Anna stopped to think.

"Yes," she said after a moment. "Even a lot. I have changed, though."

"But what is it all for?" lamented Irena. "What is it all for?"

Anna smoothed the wrinkles in the sleeper and placed it in the dresser.

"I don't know what it is all for. I do believe, however, that everything has to have a meaning, even though we may not always know what it is . . ."

"Isn't that the same as saying that nothing makes any sense?"

"Oh, no!" she retorted with deep conviction. "It's completely different."

Irena shook her head.

"No, I can't understand any of it! What good does it do for me to convince myself that everything, as you say, makes sense? What sense does all this terrible human suffering make, and everything else that is going on? What's it all for? Suffering is not at all ennobling."

"I know," whispered Anna.

"So you see! I can see it in myself. I am a much worse person now than before. And everybody else is too."

Anna suddenly thought about Julek.

"Oh, no," she disagreed. "Not everyone is worse."

"Well, maybe not!" she yielded. "But the majority are. I'm not talking about individuals. Maybe there are a few. But in general?"

Anna could not contradict her.

"Yes, you're right."

"So what sense is there in any of this," she repeated, "when thousands of the best people are dying, who could have given so much of themselves to the world, who could have done so much good? What sense does it all make, tell me that? What sense does it make?"

Anna, continuing to kneel, pushed the drawer slowly shut.

"I don't know," she replied after a moment. "I can't answer that, but I truly believe that there is an order in the world and that nothing happens without a reason."

"And what good does that do?" Irena said, shrugging her shoulders.

Anna bowed her head.

"I would just like to be better than I am," she answered quietly. "That's all!"

At the same time she thought that, of all her desires, her strongest and most deeply felt need was to be able to be proud of the person she had fallen in love with. However, she did not say so.

|||

Late in the afternoon, Julek unexpectedly appeared. Anna was glad to see him, but it turned out he had dropped by only for a moment.

"I have to be back by seven o'clock at the latest!" he announced. "And getting from here to the city is a whole journey in itself. I have to leave right away."

He was excited and overheated; one could see that he must have run very quickly from the streetcar. He took off his coat, carelessly tossing it onto the nearest armchair, and swept his tousled, matted hair from his forehead.

"You're not coming back tonight?" Anna asked.

"No!" he shook his head. "Don't wait up for me . . ."

Anna became agitated.

"You're leaving town?"

Julek took out a box of tobacco and set about rolling a cigarette.

"Something like that."

"For long?"

"I have no idea!"

"A pity," worried Anna. "Jan hasn't returned yet . . ."

Julek waved his hand and lit his cigarette.

"Janek? We'll get over it somehow!" he affirmed cheerfully and walked over to the window.

"It's you I mainly wanted to see," he said with his back turned.

He waited a moment, and when she didn't say anything, he turned around to face her. A light blush darkened his already sunburnt face.

"I wanted to tell you just one thing . . . provided you want to hear it, of course!" he added quickly.

He straddled the arms of the chair and leaned toward her.

"It's like this, you see . . ." he began. "As it turns out, I really don't know whether I will ever have the opportunity to come back . . ."

She looked at him in silence, sitting motionless, slightly rigid, with her hands clumsily clasping her knees. The bare hint of a shadow passed across her eyes.

Julek laughed out loud.

"Of course, that's just what they say. I'm sure I'll still be able to hold your child at his baptism . . ."

"Are you really going away?" she asked quietly.

"No," he denied.

In fact, he explained, he was not going anywhere. He was involved in an action to get the quickest possible armed assistance to the Jewish insurgents trapped inside the ghetto. It was not supposed to be a wide-scale action. Out of necessity, and in consideration of the entire situation of the occupation, it had to be limited to moral assistance and a demonstration of support rather than aimed at actual victory. From the very beginning, the Jewish insurgency had been doomed to annihilation and the ghetto to destruction. Under such circumstances, any kind of help might seem like a reckless increase in the number of lives lost. Nevertheless, Julek and a few others had been able to convince the leadership of one of the radical organizations that, regardless of its ultimate success, the armed Jewish resistance had to be given help from the Polish side. Preparations for the operation had been going on since yesterday. The whole plan was already drawn up, weaponry and ammunition stored, and about fifty volunteers assembled. The beginning of the operation—

breaking through to the other side behind the walls—was set for that night, from Wednesday to Thursday. That was it.

Anna sat motionless with her head bowed and her hands clasped over her knees.

"And then what?" she asked quietly.

Julek rolled another cigarette.

"What do you think?" he said, shrugging his shoulders. "We're not going to a party!"

"What you are doing is insane!" she exclaimed instinctively.

Julek lowered his dark eyes.

"Look who's talking," he said in a reproachful tone.

She looked confused. Julek got up and began to pace around the room with big steps.

"Don't think that we are doing this to make up for the various faults and crimes of our countrymen! No sacrifice, no, not any, that's not for us. It's much simpler than that. Over there people are dying, fighting for the same thing we are. For freedom! For the future! So some of us have to be with them. That much is obvious, right? It's simple solidarity, nothing more."

He glanced at his watch and stopped in front of Anna. He stood there for a moment in silence with his head slightly bowed, as if searching inside himself for the words he wanted to say.

"It's getting late," he said finally. "I have to go."

She rose, and he took her hand.

"You know," he said softly, "I never really knew my mother, I hardly remember her at all. But when I think about her, it seems to me that she must have been in her youth someone similar to you . . . just like you!"

Anna blushed and became embarrassed.

"I mean it!" he said, bending over her hand to kiss it.

When they were in the hall, she asked him whether she should tell Jan about everything.

"Do as you think best!" he finally decided.

She stood there for a moment in the hall as Julek, his boots clattering loudly, ran quickly down the stairs. When she went back inside and looked out the window of the dining room, he was already crossing the street, without his cap and with his coat thrown over his shoulder. At one point he turned around and must have spotted her watching him, for he waved. He soon disappeared around the corner.

Some time passed before she realized that she was seeing everything as though through a light fog. She was no longer able to control herself, and she let the tears flow freely down her cheeks.

|||

Malecki met Mrs. Karski in the streetcar, and they returned home together. The major's wife was very weary and worn down. She had spent the entire afternoon running about town looking for someone to buy those five hundred pairs of shoes, and when finally a customer had been found and the deal seemed done, at the last moment it turned out that the entire transport had been sold two days earlier. Who knew whether there had ever been a transport, since the seller was a middleman, third or even fourth down the line.

"I can't even begin to tell you what I feel like," she complained to Malecki. "To drag about town all day for nothing. It's enough to put a person in the grave."

Malecki listened with only half an ear, because for the last several hours he had been agonizing over what was going on at home and whether something unforeseen might have happened in his absence. So he hastened his step, slowing down only when he saw that the major's wife was having trouble keeping up with him. He became very impatient.

More or less halfway home, as they walked through a spruce grove smelling of fresh sap, they ran into Julek hurrying in the opposite direction. At first Julek moved aside as though he wanted to avoid talking to them, but Jan motioned him to stop.

"What's going on at home, Julek? Were you just there?"

"Yes," he replied briefly.

"And?"

"Everything's fine!"

Malecki sighed with relief.

"This is my brother," Jan introduced him to the major's wife.

When Mrs. Karski stated her name loudly and clearly, Julek's face darkened somewhat. Jan, for his part, realized that his brother was heading in the direction of the streetcars.

"Are you going somewhere?" he inquired. "Into town?"

"Yes."

"At this hour?"

"I'll spend the night somewhere else," Julek explained.

"I guess you'll have to!" Jan agreed.[3]

In the meantime, Mrs. Karski observed Julek closely and uneasily. So this was the man who knew her son's secrets, who knew more about him than she did herself, who could talk to him openly and about everything. She did not feel envy, but merely wanted to guess from his features and from the sound of his voice who this young Malecki was and how he had managed to win Włodek's love and admiration. But Julek was in a hurry and began to take his leave. She experienced a very strange sensation as he lowered his fair head to kiss her hand with his warm, childlike lips. He seemed to her at that moment nothing more than a shy boy, almost like her son.

"So long, old man!" said Julek, extending his hand to his brother. "Take care!"

"Good-bye," answered Jan.

Mrs. Karski could not refrain from watching him walk away. He strode quickly in long, even steps, wearing his overcoat over his shoulders so that from a distance it looked like a cape.

Tereska was still playing in front of the house. She was sitting on the steps, holding a doll dressed in a patchwork outfit sewn together from rags.

Catching sight of her mother, she ran toward her.

"Is Włodek home, dear?" the major's wife asked, kissing her.

The little girl made a petulant face.

"I don't like Włodek!"

"Why? What's happened?"

"Because he left!"

"How long ago?" she asked, becoming distressed.

Tereska shook her dark head of hair.

"Not very long ago."

But that was all she could get from the little girl. She had barely entered the apartment when she noticed that her son's coat had disappeared from its hook. Lately he had worn it only in bad weather.

"Tereska!" she called to the little girl. "Are you sure Włodek didn't say where he was going? Try to remember . . ."

Tereska, cuddling the doll in her sunburnt arms, raised a surprised eye to her mother and shook her head.

"What am I so worried about?" thought Mrs. Karski. "Nothing has happened yet." Still, she felt more and more distressed despite herself. Without taking off her hat or coat, she looked into the kitchen.

The lunch she had prepared for the children had been eaten, and Włodek must have done the dishes, because neither in the kitchen nor on the table did she see anything dirty. This raised her spirits somewhat.

"Was it a good lunch, Teresa?" she asked.

"Yes," the little girl answered very earnestly and trotted past her mother into the other room.

Mrs. Karski took off her hat. It was nearly seven now. Exactly an hour remained until curfew. "I shouldn't be so worried all the time," she thought, pressing her hands to her temples. She was about to take off her coat, when she noticed a small piece of paper on the table next to the daybed. Her heart began to pound. She immediately recognized Włodek's studious and still very schoolboyish handwriting. "Mamusia," was all he wrote, "I couldn't do otherwise."

She read this short sentence several times. At first, she was seized by the reflexive urge to run out of the house and look for Włodek. But her legs gave way beneath her. She had to sit down to keep from falling. She began reading the note once again: "Mamusia . . . " She was not thinking about anything; her mind was a complete blank. Then, as if from very far away, Tereska's quiet whisper reached her. Mechanically, she raised her head.

It was dark in the room. Tereska was standing right next to her, clutching the doll to her heart in her tiny brown arms.

"Mamusia!" She was frightened by her mother's unseeing gaze.

"What is it dear?" whispered Mrs. Karski. Tereska bowed her head. After a moment, she smoothed out the doll's patchwork dress with her tiny fingers.

"Mamusia," she began as quietly as she could. "Do you love me as much as Włodek? Tell me, do you?"

The lump in her throat prevented Mrs. Karski from answering right away. The words became stuck in her throat, and only after a long pause did she manage to whisper:

"Why yes, dearest, of course I do, just as much . . ."

|||

Malecki immediately noticed that Anna's eyes were red.

"What's wrong?" he said with concern. "Have you been crying?"

She feigned surprise.

"Of course not! Why should you think that?"

"Are you sure?" he asked doubtfully.

She laughed, and so accustomed was he to her honesty that it was easy to convince him.

"You know, I met Julek on the way here," he said, reassured. "He's taken off again somewhere. To tell the truth, it's just as well he won't be spending the night here. Last night wasn't the most pleasant . . . How's Irena?"

The strange expression on her face struck him before she was able to answer.

"What's wrong with you?" he asked with a scrutinizing look.

Anna looked confused.

"Nothing is wrong with me," she said a little uncertainly.

"But I can tell there is!"

"Really, nothing is wrong," she repeated in a more convincing tone.

Now he was sure she was not telling the truth. His egotism did not allow him to inquire further, but he was all the more offended by her evasiveness.

"You don't have to tell me if you don't want to," he said, looking at his wife harshly, "but at least don't try to convince me that nothing is wrong. I can see with my own eyes that something is!"

She only turned red and left the room without a word. He wanted to run after her, but at the last moment he restrained himself. Anna's sudden exit was so out of character that his astonishment extinguished any impulse toward anger. He stood there irresolutely, and, because he reflected now on how differently he had imagined his return home, he felt very unhappy and unjustly treated. Although he rarely disclosed his true feelings, he thought that despite everything there should always be frankness and understanding between those closest to one another.

At that evening's late supper, table conversation had trouble getting started and was maintained with difficulty. Each of the three was absorbed in his or her own thoughts, and none of them could break out of their seclusion. Fortunately, the meal was short. It was barely over when Irena went to the study, saying she wanted to retire early.

Anna wanted to take advantage of the better supply of gas in the evening to wash a few items of underclothing in the bathroom. Jan went outside for some fresh air.

Stefcio Osipowicz was still hopping about in front of the house. But at that moment his father began calling him from the third floor, and the little boy galloped upstairs with kangaroo-like leaps. In the neighboring garden the old, gray-haired man had finished watering his vegetable beds. With a slow step, slightly hunched over, he made his way home with his green watering can, this time without his grandson.

At that moment, Malecki caught the low languid voice of Mr. Piotrowski from the open ground-floor window.

"What sort of woman is that living with the Maleckis?"

"Some kike."

"How do you know that?"

"What do you mean how do I know? You only have to look at her. When did you see her? She hasn't been hanging around down here, has she?"

"No, not hanging around, but she was out on the balcony. A real looker!"

"Yes, but a kike just the same!"

"Well, what of it? You think Jewish women don't have what it takes?"

"You pig!"

Piotrowski laughed all the louder.

"But you do too, don't worry!"

"You pig!" Piotrowska repeated, but this time more softly. "I know what I have and don't have, I don't need you to tell me."

In a little while her muffled throaty laugh could be heard from inside the apartment.

Malecki lost all interest in standing in front of the house. He was about to return inside when he heard someone descending from an upper landing. In another moment the landlord, Mr. Zamojski, appeared in the doorway.

Zamojski was a solitary old widower, thin and hunched over, with a large nose that stood out a little too prominently from his small, somewhat rabbit-like face. Although when he introduced himself he never failed to pronounce his distinguished last name with care and with a certain pride, in fact he had nothing to do with the well-known Polish aristocratic family—it was only in very rare circumstances that he signed his name with a "y" instead of a "j."[4] Before the war, he had been a councillor in some ministry or other. He had a daughter whose husband had held the office of district governor, and he always referred to her as the "governor's wife." The governor's wife, along with her husband, was presently residing in Canada. The former councillor possessed a beautifully appointed apartment and, despite constant complaints about his circumstances, lived in ease and comfort. He was the only person in the building who could afford household help. His servant's name was Władek.

Spotting Malecki on the stairs, Zamojski greeted him with his customary refinement and stopped next to him.

"It's a beautiful evening," he said, breathing in the air with his long nose.

Malecki muttered something back in affirmation. He was not at all cheered by the prospect of a conversation with Zamojski, but he sensed it would not do just to walk away. He had to linger there a minute or two.

"I don't remember if the lilacs have ever bloomed as early as they have this year," Zamojski continued, very clearly pronouncing each individual word. He attached great importance to impeccable elocution.

In his opulent library he had every Polish dictionary ever published, beginning with Linde and ending with the latest principles of grammar.

"Yes, really!" agreed Malecki colorlessly and indifferently.

Zamojski did not notice this at all.

"What marvelous air!" he sighed with delectation. "Can you smell it?"

"It's the lilacs," Jan confirmed laconically.

"How wonderful they smell! What fragrance! Just like in May, a real May night."

And, as if wanting to enter into closer contact with the beauty of the night, he stood on tiptoe, his rabbit-like face upturned in rapt fascination.

Malecki began to take his leave.

"What, you're leaving already?" Zamojski fretted sincerely. "It's such a shame to stay inside on a night like this . . ."

"Unfortunately, I still have work waiting for me," Malecki explained.

Once inside, he lay down on the bed, not waiting for Anna to finish her laundry in the bathroom. He tried to read, but after a few minutes he put the book down. He did not extinguish the lamp but lay with his hands behind his head, looking up at the ceiling.

After a quarter of an hour, Anna emerged, appearing very tired.

"You know," he began, "it would be good to explain to Irena that she shouldn't show herself on the balcony. What's the point? Soon the entire house will know who we're keeping. Thanks for the advertisement!"

Anna stopped in the middle of the room.

"Has something happened?"

"No, nothing has happened!" he said irritatedly. "But the first commentaries are already appearing . . ."

"Mrs. Piotrowski?" Anna guessed. "But she already saw Irena yesterday."

"And today for a change Mr. Piotrowski saw her! Doesn't she have anything better to do than to parade out on the balcony . . ."

He only now noticed how unpleasant and irritated he sounded.

"Maybe you could tell her?" he added after a moment, this time more calmly. "She might take it better coming from you . . . After all, it's in her own best interest that she look out for herself. Not to mention us. We're a different story altogether."

He kept talking, but the more eloquent and obvious his arguments became, the more clearly he realized that all along he had been more concerned about his own peace and safety than about anything else. He had no doubt that this was abundantly clear to Anna as well. He felt too weary, however, to summon up the effort to change his tack. Anna's silence thoroughly depressed him.

"All right!" she said simply. "I'll try to take the next opportunity to talk to her."

And that was the end of the matter.

Jan fell very quickly and deeply asleep, but awoke suddenly in the middle of the night. Sleep immediately left him, and he lay there fully conscious and motionless, trying to get his bearings in the dark.

Anna slept. Next to him he heard her deep, uneven breathing. He listened for a while to its rhythm, but finally extricated himself from beneath the covers. He couldn't find his slippers in the darkness, so he went to the window barefoot and lifted the blind.

The sky over Warsaw was ablaze. From beyond the horizon live fire burst forth in several spots, while elsewhere all was darkness and quiet. High in the sky, out of range of the reflection of the blaze, the springtime stars were gaily twinkling.

As he returned from the window he bumped against a chair, and Anna immediately awoke.

"What's the matter?"

"Nothing," he replied softly. "I just wanted to get a drink of water."

He located the carafe on the table and poured himself a glass. He drank thirstily, for his throat was completely parched. In another moment he had climbed back under the covers, but he was not the least bit sleepy. It was barely one o'clock, and he had the whole long night ahead of him.

Since Anna did not move for some time, he was certain she had fallen asleep again. Then suddenly he felt next to him, at barely an arm's width away, the light trembling of her body. For a moment he stopped breathing, then raised himself up on one elbow.

"Ania!" he whispered, leaning over his wife. "What's the matter?"

She did not reply, but her attempts to stifle her sobbing now shook her whole upper body.

"Ania, Ania," he said, putting his arm around her. "Ania dearest . . ."

She lay with her face pressed to her pillow. He was about to turn her toward him when she turned over herself and, although her thoughts were very far away from her husband, leaned against his chest and broke out into loud sobbing, like a child.

Chapter 4 ꠸ꠐ꠸

ALL THROUGH THE NEXT DAY the battle in the ghetto continued un-
abated. The insurgents defended themselves ferociously and strategically,
contesting every street and individual housing block. The Nazis called in detachments of Latvian, Lithuanian, and Ukrainian soldiers to aid them. They
loved to get other nationalities to do their dirty work, breeding in this way
mutual hatred among them.

In those parts of the ghetto that had not embraced the rebellion and were
not taking part in the battle, things were peaceful. Smugglers taking food into
the Jewish quarter reported that life there went on as usual. In just a few days
those people, too, having deluded themselves with hope to the very end, were
going to die, and their homes were going to burn. Just as during the liquidation of the so-called little ghetto in the spring of the previous year, the Germans had laid a special railway spur into the Jewish section. One after another
the trains pulled up, and the freight cars were loaded with defenseless people.
The gas chambers of the concentration camp at Majdanek absorbed ever more
transports of people.

Here, however, as the battle and resistance raged, the fires encompassed
an ever greater number of houses. In the apartment houses that had caught fire
first, the flames were slowly dying out. On the Jewish side of Bonifraterska
Street, beyond the brick walls, rose the skeletons of burnt-out buildings.

The corner house that had caught fire the previous evening was still
burning. It was probably abandoned by its tenants and already stripped of its
furniture, for the fire consumed the structure very slowly. During the night
barely two floors had burned away; now flames were licking out of the empty
windows of the second floor.

The largest fires could be seen in the Muranów district and farther off toward Powązki. The wind changed direction often, and a considerable part of

downtown was filled with the stench of the fire. An enormous black cloud hung over Warsaw. Still, in the city lively traffic and a holiday atmosphere prevailed. It was Maundy Thursday.

||||

Malecki left for the city in the morning at the usual time. He was not to have a day off until Good Friday. However, when he turned up at August 6 Street,[1] where the firm's small two-room headquarters were located, it turned out after the preceding day's feverish excitement there was not much to do. Additionally, the work most in need of tending to was not going well. The firm's owner, Wolański, also an architect and Malecki's acquaintance from before the war, had not yet come to work.

In one of the two rooms, called the commons area (the other, where Wolański and Malecki had their desks, was called "administration"), a lively discussion had been taking place for some time. When Malecki, intrigued by the raised voices, looked in, he found he had stepped into the middle of a heated debate.

In the commons area he found four people: the administrative secretary Stefa, an attractive platinum blonde whose curled eyelashes and plucked eyebrows gave her face the expression of childish surprise; the typist Marta; the office boy Bartkowiak; and a young man, the only one who was not among the firm's employees. He was a tall blond with an elongated head and deep-set eyes placed on a birdlike, somewhat predatory face.

Malecki was acquainted with the young man, since Zalewski—or Zygmunt, as Stefa called him—had lately been paying frequent visits to August 6 Street. Before the war he had studied law, but now, among other interests, he traded in gold and hard currency.

When Malecki entered the commons area, Zalewski was sitting on a table, vigorously gesticulating.

"I'm telling you that at least in this one instance we can be grateful to Hitler. He's relieved us of the whole burdensome and, let's frankly admit, unpleasant and dirty business. Now there won't even be a Jewish question. If Hitler hadn't done it now, we'd have had to see to the liquidation of the Jews after the war ourselves. It's one problem less, that's for sure! And all these so-called humanitarian concerns," he said, directing himself to Marta, who was sitting in front of her Underwood, "have nothing to do with the present situation!

Poland has to be free of Jews: it's our *raison d'état*. That's one thing. The other thing is that we don't have any reason to feel sorry for the Jews. They don't feel sorry for us! If only they had the chance, any one of them would gladly shoot in the head the first Pole he met. If the Jews came to power, then they'd really show us what they're capable of!"

He spoke quickly, fervently, and with an unshakable conviction, with the voice of a man accustomed to frequent speechifying and public debate. Stefa, batting her long eyelashes, gazed at Zalewski with evident admiration. Bartkowiak's face also registered an attitude of approval. Only Marta had turned away from the speaker. Her dark, sleekly combed-back hair accentuated her youthful expression. She sat bent over her machine.

Noticing Malecki, Zalewski turned toward him.

"Am I wrong, sir?"

Malecki found himself in an unpleasant situation. He did not have the slightest desire to enter into the discussion. However, after Zalewski's question, everyone's gaze turned directly on him. Even Marta lifted her head. She was very pale, and her mouth trembled.

He felt he had to say something.

"I didn't hear the entire conversation," he began slowly, "but what you say doesn't sound original . . ."

"Of course not!" Zalewski agreed with satisfaction. "The Polish nation long ago began to understand what the Jews are like . . ."

"Before the war, similar thoughts were popular among our fascists," Malecki observed.

Zalewski frowned.

"You mean the nationalists?"

"Isn't it the same thing?"

"No!" he retorted sharply.

Squinting his eyes, he aggressively appraised Malecki.

"We know very well what circles try to discredit us by pinning the label of fascist on us, but after the war we'll explain to these gentlemen what the difference is."

"In concentration camps, no doubt?" put in Marta.

Zalewski was temporarily at a loss, but quickly regained his composure.

"If it comes to that, then yes!" he replied sharply. "Precisely there and nowhere else we'll show the Jews and Communists who we are . . ."

Suddenly the room fell silent. Stefa, a little unsure whether Zygmunt had not said too much, took out a compact and, still batting her eyelashes, began to swipe a powder-puff across her pretty face. Marta grew even paler. As far as Malecki was concerned, he would have been happiest to extricate himself from this unpleasant exchange.

Then Marta arose.

"No one knows how long it will be to the end of the war," she said in a trembling voice, "so to save time I will tell you who you are right now!"

Zalewski smiled ironically.

"Go ahead, I'm listening."

"You're common criminals!" she said straight into his face.

He made a movement as if to interrupt her, but she cast at him such a baleful look that he remained silent.

"You're criminals, the whole lot of you!" she repeated even more loudly. "I wish I could just despise you, but that's not good enough. You're a disgrace to each and every one of us who calls himself a Pole, you sick bastards!" she cried with a passion unexpected from one usually so calm and self-controlled.

As she left the room, Malecki ran into the hall after her.

"Marta!" he called out.

She was hurriedly putting on her coat.

"Yes?" she replied coldly.

"I wanted to say that . . ."

"Yes, I can imagine what you wanted to say," she interrupted him. "No doubt you wanted to communicate to me that I was right?"

"Of course!"

The woman gave him a sardonic smile.

"Too bad you didn't say so in there," she said, indicating the other room.

Malecki was taken aback.

"It seems to me . . ." he began, attempting to justify himself.

" . . . that you adequately expressed your point of view?" she interrupted him again. "Of course, you expressed your point of view most eloquently. So eloquently, in fact, that I feel relieved of the obligation to call it by its true name. But that's no longer important. I would be greatly obliged if you would be so kind as to communicate to Mr. Wolański that as of today I am no longer working for him."

That was the last thing he expected. Marta had been working there for only a couple of weeks. He knew that her material situation was difficult and that she very much needed this job, which did not pay at all badly.

"Please reconsider!" he tried to persuade her.

"I already did," she replied decisively.

When Wolański appeared in the office an hour later, Malecki recounted the entire affair to him.

"I couldn't make her see the light," he concluded. "It was no, no, and no."

The broad-shouldered, ruddy-faced Wolański, dressed elegantly in a light-colored spring suit, merely waved his hand.

"Let her go to hell! There's a hundred more to take her place, never fear."

Malecki felt the need to come to Marta's defense.

"You have to admit that she was a decent girl."

"Sure, I admit it!" he said, grimacing. "But a hysteric nonetheless."

"And Zalewski . . ."

"That scum!" Wolański said curtly. "But, between you and me, the guy has a point. You know, I don't support such methods . . . In no way do I consider myself a fascist sympathizer, but what's true is true. Hitler is solving our Jewish problem in his own way, barbarically, but decisively. Speaking of Jews, did you know the Liliens?"

Malecki leaned over his desk and began to study the proposed plans of a real estate transaction.

"Yes, I did," he blurted out.

"Can you believe I saw Miss Lilien yesterday on Marszałkowska Street."

"Yesterday?" Malecki asked in amazement.

"Or maybe the day before. I can't remember anymore. But it was definitely her. Do you happen to know what's going on with her?"

"I've no idea," he replied.

Since there wasn't a thing to do in the office, Wolański wanted to drag Malecki out for a late breakfast. One thing he liked was to eat and drink well.

"I'm buying!" he declared when Malecki tried to beg off.

But Malecki really didn't want to go. He said it was because of a lack of time, so they left the office together and parted ways soon afterward on Savior Square. Wolański hailed a passing rickshaw.[2]

"Won't you reconsider?" he asked, turning once again to Malecki. "Hop on in, it's worth celebrating the beautiful day, and it's Maundy Thursday to boot . . ."

"Some other time!" Malecki retorted.

Wolański laughed.

"There'll always be another time! But as you wish . . ." he said.

Wolański gave the driver—a pale, frail boy—the address of a stylish wartime locale on Mazowiecka Street. The boy nodded his head and urged his heavy bicycle into motion. Stooping and with effort, he began to guide his vehicle into the depths of Marszałkowska Street with the man comfortably ensconced on the seat up front.

In that same direction a heavy, dark, swollen cloud of smoke hung over the Saxon Garden. Some of the passersby stopped on the sidewalk and gazed off that way.

Malecki crossed to the other side of the street and stopped at the streetcar stand. He decided to take advantage of his free time by heading out to the Makowski family in Mokotów.

The building in which they lived had one of the highest numbers on Puławska Street and was located in the far reaches of Mokotów. It was a large and modern cooperative building, its smooth, monotonous plane uninterrupted but for the rows of wide windows.

Malecki remembered the number of the Makowskis' apartment, but he stopped at the gate to check the tenant list in order to find out which stairwell he had to enter.

Suddenly the doorman peeped out of his room.

"Who are you looking for?" he asked in a lower-class Warsaw accent.

"The Makowskis," Malecki explained. "What stairwell would that be?"

The watchman, a short and gloomy man pushing fifty, observed him carefully.

"No one's in number seventeen," he muttered.

"Have they gone out?" Malecki said, beginning to worry.

Then he recalled that Mrs. Makowski's mother, a frail old lady who rarely went out because of her rheumatism, also lived with them, and he asked about her.

The watchman shrugged.

"I'm telling you there isn't anyone there."

After a pause he added with distaste:

"The apartment's been sealed; there's no point in going there."

Malecki shuddered.

"What do you mean?"

"Just what I said."

"What happened?" he began to interrogate him. "When?"

"Late last night," the man replied.

Malecki was silent for a while. There was every indication that the detention of the entire Makowski family was closely connected to Tuesday's incident with Irena. The agents must not have been satisfied with their modest blackmail and had come back for more. Unable to get anything, they must have used the situation to show themselves to advantage to their superiors at Gestapo headquarters. Malecki would have preferred to make certain, but to any more confidential questions the doorman answered merely with a shrug of his shoulders and a gloomy expression that in itself said much. He did not trust him, that much was clear, probably taking him for an informer. Finally, escorted out of the entryway under the hostile gaze of the doorman, he went out onto the street with a sense of shame and directed himself toward town, still enveloped in clouds of smoke.

More or less halfway along Puławska Street he observed the following incident.

Along the left-hand side of this stretch of Puławska were old tenement buildings and wooden shacks leaning toward ruin, gloomy warrens inhabited by the poorest of the poor. The poverty and filth here were terrible, all the more apparent in that on the opposite side of the street there rose bright, clean, modern apartment blocks. Behind the shacks stretched miserable-looking garden plots, as yet barren and gray, and for the most part given over to potatoes.

A confused shouting reached Malecki's ears from behind the shacks, and, along with several other passersby, he came to a stop.

A group of screaming children was chasing a small, stooped street urchin across a potato field.

"A Jew, a Jew!" the shrill, childish voices could be heard shouting.

A whole group of them was pursuing and throwing rocks and dirt-clods at the fleeing boy, who was running with all his waning strength. He started to dash to one side, but another group of children came running from that direction, whistling and hollering, and so he rushed straight ahead toward the street.

Small and dark, wearing rags through which the yellowish-blue skin of his emaciated body showed, he ran at full speed from behind a wooden shack straight out onto the sidewalk. Dazed and disoriented by the street, by the streetcar passing by at that moment, and by the throngs of motionless people standing there, he came to a stop. And that was his fatal move.

From a distance of no more than four or five paces a young, well-built German soldier came toward him. The pursuing children evidently saw the soldier from a distance and immediately dispersed across the fields. A few hid behind the houses and peered out furtively.

The boy noticed the approaching soldier only at the last moment. He shuddered and tried to pull his head down between his bony shoulders, but he no longer tried to escape. With motionless eyes wide open, he watched the approaching broad-shouldered silhouette. Nor did he cry out or twitch when the soldier grabbed him by the scruff of the neck like a puppy, bent his head straight back, and looked him in the face. The boy stared back at him intently with the same frozen, unseeing expression.

"*Jude?*" the German asked, without a trace of anger.

The little Jew did not reply. The soldier continued to hold him by the neck, while with his other hand he reached for his sidearm and, without even aiming, fired two shots, one right after the other.

|||

Meanwhile, the house where the Maleckis lived had been taken over with pre-holiday bustle since early morning. From the Osipowiczes' apartment on the third floor, the noisy pounding of mortar and pestle could be heard. Mr. Zamojski's servant Władek was out beating rugs and wall hangings in front of the house, while Mrs. Piotrowski, her skirt tucked up above her knees, was washing the windows and scrubbing the sills.[3] Wacek Piotrowski was running barefoot about the courtyard waving a pine branch, shouting unintelligible, fantastic words. Stefcio Osipowicz soon joined him. For a moment he stood in the doorway chewing a piece of bread and butter, observing his comrade attentively. But then, in a single bound, he leaped down off the stairs and, in his strange kangaroo-like way, began to hop over to Wacek. A moment later his father, an assistant professor of mathematics, came running downstairs, thin, pale, and frantic. Chased out of the house by the kitchen clatter, he had taken a book, notebook, and pencil to find refuge among the spruces. No sooner had he sat down and set to work than the shouts of young Piotrowski reached him. Arranging a handkerchief over his head because of the beating sun, he set off at a quick trot in the direction of the sandy field beyond the house.

"Wacek!" Mrs. Piotrowski shouted from the windowsill. "Will you shut your trap! Do you want a spanking?"

The little boy at first cowered in terror, but rapidly recovered. Mrs. Piotrowski, her huge, white calves showing from under her tucked-up skirt, had scarcely bent over the washbasin full of soapsuds when her son suddenly squealed frightfully, jumped up, and, waving a branch, rushed out into the street with Stefcio Osipowicz bounding on his tail.

Mr. Piotrowski, still sleepy and wearing an unbuttoned shirt, came outside. Lazily stretching his arms, he yawned, ran his hands through his thick, tousled hair, and hiked up his loose pants. At the same time, he glanced up toward the Maleckis' balcony. It was empty, and the windows were covered by a dark blind.

Piotrowski stretched once again and came down off the stoop.

"Hey, old lady!" he said, standing before the window. "Gimme a cigarette . . ."

"Old lady yourself! Just listen to him!" she cut him off derisively. "Get it yourself!"

He shrugged his shoulders and yawned.

"Oh, come on and bring me a cigarette! I don't feel like dragging myself back into the apartment."

"What else do you have to do? Can't you see I'm busy?"

"Great God Almighty!" scowled Piotrowski. "So much chatter and so little action!"

She soon got down off the windowsill and returned after a moment with a cigarette.

"Here, you lazy bum!" she said, handing it to him through the window. "You'd be better off helping me than loafing about the house all day . . ."

He laughed cheerfully and went up to Władek who was cleaning a large Hucul[4] carpet with a brush.

"Got a light, Władek?"

Władek nodded, put down his brush, and reached into his tidy vest for a lighter. As he lit Piotrowski's cigarette, he took one for himself from his silver cigarette case. Władek attached great importance to externals. He wore freshly ironed trousers, and his light-colored hair was carefully slicked back.

Piotrowski inhaled the smoke and again glanced in the direction of the Maleckis' balcony. The morning sun in its full glory illuminated the second-floor windows. He leaned against the carpet-cleaning bar, and in this way was able to observe the entire building.

"So what's up, Władek?" he asked.

"The holidays!" Władek said laconically, looking down at his carefully groomed fingernails.

"Will you be having a party?" Piotrowski asked interestedly, thinking, of course, of Zamojski.

Władek understood what he meant.

"Fat chance of that!" he said, lightly grimacing. "We haven't got any money."

"Oh, really?"

"Nobody pays their rent."

"I pay regularly," Piotrowski reminded him. "You can't say I don't."

"Yes, you do!" Władek admitted. "But that Karski lady owes us for four months, and Osipowicz for three!"

"So toss them out!" Piotrowski advised matter-of-factly.

Władek brushed a speck of dust off his vest.

"That's easy enough to say. But one needs to experience life in someone else's shoes before passing judgment. We would never do such a thing . . ."

"No, of course you wouldn't," Piotrowski muttered, casually searching the windows of the second floor.

"We'd never do such a thing," Władek repeated in a tone of calm and conscious pride.

|||

Irena had slept very badly that night. She awoke numerous times from a light sleep and each time became irksomely fully conscious. She did not try to get up, however, and only once pulled back the blind.

In the distance the night was ablaze, so she quickly lowered the blind and lay with eyes closed, engulfed by a silence and darkness that did not lull her to sleep. Every once in a while, the sounds of gunshots and the stronger shocks of explosions reached her from far away. She did not fall deeply asleep until the first light of dawn as it was growing gray outside and the first sparrows were beginning to chirp.

She awoke in the darkened room amid sparkling shafts of sunlight with a splitting headache, feeling weary and beaten down, poisoned by thoughts that she tried to banish and repress. Her mind was a complete blank, nor did a single recollection disturb her dull stupor. She was paralyzed and silenced by worries so immense that they drowned out all suffering, hope, and fear. She lay in this torturous void for a long time. The only sounds that made it through to her consciousness were the sharply penetrating sounds from the courtyard—the pounding of the mortar and pestle, the beating of carpets, and the shouting of children at play.

She also heard Anna moving about the apartment. At one point, it even seemed that she had come up to the door to listen to what was going on inside. Irena did not budge, pretending to be asleep, afraid that Anna would enter, and she breathed a sigh of relief when she heard the front door slam. She listened for a while, but the apartment remained silent.

When she got up and raised the blind, bright sunlight rushed in and flooded the entire room. At first she felt blinded. She shielded her eyes and only then saw Anna slowly and heavily crossing the street with a shopping bag.

Two men were conversing in front of the house next to the carpet rack. One of them was the same man who had spotted her on the balcony the preceding afternoon. She quickly noticed that Piotrowski, while leaning against the carpet rack, constantly glanced up at the window in which she stood. She hastily withdrew and stood in such a way as to observe the courtyard without herself being seen. But Piotrowski, his hands shoved into his pockets, kept looking up at the balcony so intently that she was unsure that he had not seen her after all, so she withdrew inside the room. The incident kept gnawing at her and, when after a while she again heard the sounds of someone beating a carpet, she drew near to the balcony.

Piotrowski was nowhere to be seen. There was only Władek rhythmically and methodically beating a rug, so she moved closer, but instantly pulled back with a start that surprised even her.

Piotrowski was lying sprawled out on the grass in front of the balcony, which he was intently observing. Such a wave of anxiety came over her that she hurriedly began to get dressed, forgetting even to wash up.

When Anna returned soon afterward, Irena ran out into the hall to meet her. "It's good you've returned," she cried out. "We have to have a talk . . ."

And, without letting Anna get a word in edgewise, she began incoherently to explain why it would be better if she did not stay in Bielany any longer but left immediately.

Anna took fright.

"Has something happened?"

"No, no!" Irena said. "But just take a look outside in the courtyard . . ."

Anna obeyed.

"Do you see him?" Irena asked, remaining inside the room.

At that moment, Władek was pulling his rug off the carpet rack.

"That's our landlord's butler," Anna explained, still uncomprehending.

"What about the other one, on the grass?"

"There's no one there!"

Irena drew closer. It seemed, indeed, that Piotrowski had left. In a calmer voice, she again related the entire event. Anna tried to reassure her. She spoke with such conviction and so rationally that Irena easily allowed herself to be convinced.

"Are you sure it's not dangerous?"

"Absolutely!" Anna assured her, although she was a little concerned herself. Irena sighed with relief.

"That's good, because I had already convinced myself I would have to go into hiding again."

"Don't even talk about it," Anna repeated.

"To tell the truth," mused Irena, "I don't have anywhere to go. I have no one."

During their late breakfast she returned to the subject once more.

"You know," she told Anna, who was sitting close by with some sewing, "I don't know what I am more afraid of: death itself or this constant uncertainty."

Anna, who had been thinking about Julek, did not immediately reply. After a moment, she responded, bending over the baby's sleeper.

"It seems to me that a person does not fear death if he believes in some kind of values that are . . . in something that is larger than himself . . ."

Irena regarded her closely.

"Are you talking about God?"

"No!" Anna replied sincerely. "I was not thinking about God, only about people."

|||

Since cutting a pattern always caused Anna the greatest difficulty and since she had a piece of flannel sufficient for at least two more little sleepers, she decided to take advantage of Mrs. Karski's expertise and to drop in on her with some questions on how to cut the material. Warning Irena that she would be alone for half an hour, she headed upstairs.

Mrs. Karski opened the door herself.

"I have a big favor to ask of you . . ." Anna began.

She was caught off guard, however, by the unexpected appearance of the major's wife. At first glance, in the half shadow of the hallway, Mrs. Karski seemed to her a completely different woman, at least a dozen years older. Her face was dark and sunken, her eyes disproportionately large and aflame with hidden suffering.

Thinking that Mrs. Karski was ill, she was about to beg her pardon for the intrusion when Mrs. Karski embraced her warmly.

"It's good that you've come. Please come in."

As they crossed into the living room, Tereska immediately poked her head out of the other room. Mrs. Karski went up to her.

"Go and play now, Teresa dear," she said, stroking her head. "Mamusia wants to talk with the lady now."

The little girl pursed her lips sourly.

"What about me?"

"Later, dear. Go and play by yourself now."

"But I always have to play by myself," the little girl responded.

However, she did leave. Mrs. Karski stood at the door for a moment, and then finally sat down opposite Anna. In the full light, her face still wore a very harried expression.

"It's good that you've come," she repeated with deliberate reflection. "I had actually wanted to stop by to see you. I wanted to . . ."

She lowered her head, and only after a moment directed her dark eyes toward Anna.

"Please tell me . . ." she began with pronounced hesitation. "Perhaps you know . . . where I could find your brother-in-law, Julek?"

Anna blushed lightly.

"You don't know?"

She shook her head.

"Doesn't he come around anymore?

"No, he doesn't," she answered quietly.

"Oh, I see!" the major's wife whispered to herself.

The silence lingered.

"Did Włodek want to see Julek?" Anna asked.

"No," she said. "Włodek didn't come home last night."

Anna shuddered.

"What do you mean he didn't come home?"

Mrs. Karski rose, took a sheet of paper from her handbag lying on the table, and without a word handed it to Anna. She read it once, then a second time. The major's wife suddenly leaned toward her and took her hand.

"I beg you, if you know anything at all about Julek, please tell me. They must be together, I'm sure of it. I'm not going to get in anyone's way. I only want to know, I just want to know where my son is, what he wants to die for, nothing else . . ."

Anna was certain that Włodek had taken part in the same operation as Julek. Still she hesitated, not knowing whether she had the right to reveal the secret that had been entrusted to her. Mrs. Karski sensed this.

"I implore you," she said, squeezing her hand even more firmly.

There was so much worry and suffering in her voice that Anna decided to tell her. Mrs. Karski listened calmly and in silence. Her face became gray, and her eyes fell into shadows.

"So, that's how it is," she said, as Anna fell silent. "I shall never see him again . . ."

"Maybe they didn't go together." Anna whispered.

Mrs. Karski shook her head.

"No, no. I'm sure they're together! What more can I do . . ."

She got up and pressed her tiny, narrow hands to her temples.

"What more can I do . . ." she repeated softly. "In Poland mothers know that in raising their sons to be honest men, most often they are just preparing them for death. But why didn't he tell me?" she blurted out in despair. "I wouldn't have stopped him . . . How could I have stopped him?"

III

In the afternoon the sound of very loud explosions from the direction of the city began to reach Bielany more frequently. At such a considerable distance it was difficult to tell what triggered the detonations, whether dynamite or incendiary bombs. Each explosion must have started a new fire, for within a few moments after each one, a thick, black column of smoke rose up toward the sky above the ghetto.

In the Piotrowskis' kitchen an Easter loaf was baking and a ham was cooking. The smell of cabbage stew filled the entire apartment stairwell. Mrs. Piotrowski, red from the heat and dressed now in a shirt and a colorful slip, was finishing up the housecleaning in moments when she did not have to watch the oven, running back and forth between the kitchen and the living room. She wanted to finish everything before evening.

"Great God Almighty . . ." she cried as an explosion, stronger than the rest, shook the ground. "They're really pounding them!"

She approached the window, and immediately her attention was drawn to a small group of people gathered on the sidewalk beyond the corner in front of Makarczyński's house.

"Józef!" she said, looking in on the other room. "Look, something's happened over at Makarczyński's."

"What if it has?" he responded, remaining on the bed.

"Look at that bunch of people down there!"

He reluctantly got up and peered out.

"Bah, a bunch . . . there's only a couple."

"What do mean, a couple?" she said with indignation. "Count them: six, seven . . . Look, even Zamojski's butler is there."

Władek indeed was standing among the conversing bystanders, but Piotrowski was not at all moved.

"So what?" he muttered, shrugging.

"Oh, my Lord!" she said anxiously. "Can't you see something has happened? Go and see what."

"Go yourself," he drawled lazily.

"Dear God Almighty! Can't you see I'm not dressed!? I'm asking you like one human being to another."

The excited gestures of the gathering finally interested even Piotrowski, and he pulled on a sports coat and hat and went out. While walking across the courtyard, he took a look up at the Maleckis' balcony.

In the meantime, his wife had run into the kitchen to stir her stew. She checked to see whether her loaf was turning brown and quickly returned to the living room. Piotrowski had already joined the crowd.

After about ten minutes he was back.

"Well, what was it?" she asked excitedly, meeting him in the doorway. "What took you so long? What's happened?"

"Oh, I don't know," he said, tossing his hat on the bed. "They're just gabbing."

"What do mean just gabbing? What are they gabbing about?"

"Oh, the Gestapo showed up somewhere on Lisowska Street . . ."

"You don't mean it!" she said in fright. "When, just now? Did they arrest anyone?"

"Oh, supposedly some Jews," he replied indifferently.

His wife turned red and lost her power of speech, so much did this news discomfit her. She finally regained her composure.

"Józek!" she shouted out energetically. "Keep an eye on the oven. I'll be right back."

She opened a wardrobe, pulled out a dress, and hastily began to put it on. Piotrowski screwed up his face.

"Where are you off to?"

"To Zamojski's," she answered briskly, pulling on her stockings.

He shrugged.

"What is it now?"

"What do you mean what is it?" she said, straightening up, all red and sweaty. "Don't you see what's going on here? Am I supposed to sit here on my hands until they wipe us all out for some damned Jewish bitch?[5] Not on your life! I'm not one to go to the Gestapo, I don't want to have anyone's blood on my hands, but if I don't go then someone else will."

Already dressed, she ran into the kitchen and peered into the oven. Her loaf was turning the proper shade of brown. She stirred the stew and returned to the living room. She straightened her hair, powdered her flushed face, and picked up her handbag.

"Józek!" she reminded him once again as she stood in the doorway, "If I'm not back in a quarter of an hour, then take out the bread and give the stew a stir. Don't forget!"

"Yeah, sure!" he muttered.

He took off his coat and lay down on the bed, propping his feet up against the high metal rail in his favorite position.

In the meantime, his wife had vociferously persuaded Władek that she had to see the councillor on a very important and urgent matter and was already standing in Zamojski's study. It was a large room with an immense carpet and a heavy desk in the center, surrounded by massive bookshelves. On the walls, in opulently gilded frames, hung old-fashioned portraits. The curtains draping the windows and the deep club chairs created an atmosphere of calm and quiet.

Zamojski was at that moment reading *Pan Tadeusz*,[6] and Piotrowska's unexpected visit was most inopportune. From experience he knew that the visits of tenants never augured anything good. However, his good upbringing caused him immediately to rise from his chair and to arrange his rabbit-like face into a pleasant smile. Only the councillor's large nose betrayed his dissatisfaction.

Piotrowska sank into an armchair and, wiping her sweaty brow with her handkerchief, immediately got down to business.

"You know, sir, I'm an honest person and you can search the whole world over for anyone else who pays her rent so regularly . . ."

Zamojski nodded politely, while Piotrowska breathed deeply and again reached for her handkerchief.

"Just so!" she affirmed her previous statement. "So I have the right to speak up when something's going on in this building that's not right, don't I?"

Zamojski's nose grew imperceptibly longer.

"Yes, councillor, I know what I'm talking about. I'm not just blowing hot air. In the times we live in, can one allow the foolhardiness of some to endanger the lives of others? Can one be allowed to behave, if I may put it that way, antisocially?"

"But . . ." Zamojski blurted out.

"But nothing!" Piotrowska went on the attack. "What would you say, sir, if you knew that here, in your own house, under this very roof, someone is harboring, if you'll pardon the expression, Jews?"

Zamojski twitched, and his nose grew distinctly longer.

"I don't know anything about it," he declared in a weak voice.

"But I do!" exclaimed Piotrowska, fanning herself with her handkerchief. "And the Maleckis do, too."

Zamojski was still recovering from his first unpleasant reaction.

"Just a moment, my dear lady," he said, assuming a matter-of-fact tone. "If I understand you correctly, you mean to say that in the Maleckis' apartment there are people who . . ."

"Not people, but some Jewish woman!" she said, dispelling all doubt.

Zamojski rubbed his nose with the back of his hand.

"Now wait a second . . . how do you know that that lady . . ."

"Because I have eyes!" she said, becoming indignant. "I'm an expert, if you don't mind my saying so. I only need to look once."

The soft leather armchair was growing warm beneath her, causing her to creep forward and sit on its very edge.

"You know, councillor, I am a Pole," she said, wiping her sweaty brow, "and I won't go running to the Germans with it, never you fear . . ."

"Of course not!" Zamojski spread his arms wide in order to emphasize how far he was from making any such assumption.

"Well of course not! But we can't just live here like this on top of a volcano. There are little children living here!"

"Yes, yes," Zamojski interrupted her. "I will have a chat with Mr. and Mrs. Malecki. We have to clear this thing up. Perhaps there has been some misunderstanding?"

"There is no misunderstanding, sir," she retorted, offended. "I'm a responsible person. I don't make accusations lightly."

"Of course not, of course not," he said quickly, trying to mollify her. "And does anyone other than yourself know about this?"

"I really don't know," she shrugged. "That's not my concern. In any case, I haven't been gabbing it about. But you know what people are like . . . They like to know what's chirping in the grass."

"Of course, of course" he agreed. "I'll clear this whole thing up."

He ushered her into the front hall and said good-bye in Władek's presence with such elaborate courtesy that she returned home reassured and satisfied. But no sooner had she crossed the threshold of her apartment than the suspicious smell of something burning hit her. Overcome by an evil premonition, she rushed into the kitchen. A cheerful flame blazed under one of the burners, while the smell of scorched cabbage issued from the pot of stew. Then she looked in the oven and wrung her hands at the sight of the blackened Easter loaves, and anger quickly replaced her sorrow.

She burst into the main room at a dash. The sight of her husband sprawled lackadaisically on the bed sent her into a frenzy.

"You lazy good-for-nothing!" she yelled. "I told you, you son of a bitch, to keep an eye on the bread. Now you'll have shit to eat!"

By the time she had finished getting the rage out of her system, Piotrowski abruptly hopped up from the bed, grabbed her by the wrists, and pushed her against the wall.

"You're hurting me!" she wailed in fright. "What's gotten into you, Józek?"

"I'll tell you what's gotten into me," he said, squeezing her wrists still more firmly. "Look, you cow! You're never going to poke your nose into other people's goddamned business again, are you?"

"But it's you I'm thinking about, Józek!" she said, trying to defend herself. "It's you I'm afraid for."

"Are you?" he asked.

Her eyes filled with tears of pain and humiliation, and at the same time a familiar faintness came over her. She was defenseless against this man. For five years, day after day, in good times and in bad, he had defeated her with his body, his alcohol-soaked breath, and his voice.

"Well?" he asked again.

She only shook her head.

"You won't?"

"No," she whispered.

"So don't forget!" he said through his teeth and pushed her away from him so forcibly that she stumbled over the threshold, knocked against a nearby chair, and fell down. Piotrowski threw his shoulders back angrily and with a contemptuous kick slammed the door shut behind him.

It was several moments before she slowly got up and, stifling her sobs, began to rub her swollen hands. Suddenly she noticed that in falling she had torn her stockings in the most visible spot, right in front. They were French silk stockings purchased barely a week ago at the Kercelak[7] market for a hefty price, even for such a smuggler as she. Now she began crying in earnest. Through her tears, bitterness, and anger she began screaming: "May you shrivel up and die, you Jewish ape, you damned Jewish bitch! I work and I slave and then because of the likes of you . . . ! Maybe there really is no God . . ."

|||

Malecki returned home on foot, wanting to quiet his nerves. He had to traverse the whole city, taking a route that wound for several kilometers, but neither his being in motion nor his weariness could rid him of the thoughts assailing him.

Everywhere Warsaw throbbed with movement and din. The spring day was drawing to a close, but the stores and shops were all still open. The lively pulse of the upcoming holidays was evident in the shop windows displaying their gaudy wartime fare and in the crowds doing their last-minute shopping. The sidewalks were crawling with all manner of street vendors noisily hawking their wares. Baskets of violets, marsh marigolds, and primroses stood on the corners. The air smelled of spring, and the sky, too, would have been truly vernal, had its bright and delicate azure not been eclipsed by the gray trails of smoke. Above the ghetto rose a black and nearly motionless cloud of smoke, like a monstrous giant. Echoes from the relentless shooting multiplied among the houses, and explosions shook the earth one after the other.

By the time he reached Żoliborz, Malecki felt so tired that he decided to board a streetcar. Even so, he arrived home much later than he had planned that morning.

On hearing him arrive, Irena looked out into the hall. She noticed right away that he was missing the suitcase he had promised.

"Oh, you didn't bring my things," she fretted.

"Unfortunately not," he replied reluctantly.

"Didn't you go to the Makowskis?" Anna inquired.

Irritated by the inquisition, he answered in a roundabout way and disappeared into the bathroom, saying he had to wash up. Once there, he took much longer than the situation required. He washed his face, which he was not in the habit of doing during the day, scrubbed his hands, and even trimmed his fingernails, which suddenly seemed to him overly long. Finally, sensing that he was prolonging his absence more than decency allowed, he combed his hair and opened the door.

Both women were sitting in the study. Irena was looking at a book of Breughel prints and didn't glance up when Jan entered. Avoiding the inquisitive gaze of his wife, he sat off to one side.

"I did go to the Makowskis'," he began.

Irena bent over one of the reproductions.

"And?" she asked indifferently.

He spent several moments looking for the right words.

"Weren't they at home?" Anna asked.

"No."

"That's terrible!" she fussed. "Now you'll have to go there all over again tomorrow."

"No need to bother," he replied. "The Makowskis have been arrested and their apartment has been sealed."

Irena sat motionless over her album.

"When were they arrested?" she asked after a while in the same indifferent tone.

"Late Tuesday night."

"That didn't take long." Her voice betrayed a slight trace of irony. "Were all of them taken?"

"Yes, all of them."

Two distant explosions broke the silence so violently that the window panes rattled in their frames.

"Did you have a lot of things there?" Jan asked.

She shrugged.

"Nothing important. Just stuff."

Jan quickly began to explain that that wasn't what he meant. He wanted to know whether among her personal effects there might have been anything compromising.

"I don't think so," she considered. "There was just a photograph of my father, and a couple of snapshots of my mother."

"No letters?"

She finally looked up at him. "No, don't worry. I didn't save any of your letters."

He let the gibe pass without comment.

"And those two who came to your place, did they know your current name?"

"Of course! What do you think?"

"Great! That complicates everything. If those were the same people who caused the arrest of the Makowskis . . ."

"You simply have to get new documents," Anna broke in.

Irena took a look at the old-fashioned ring she wore on her finger.

"I can sell this. It's all I have left! But it won't bring in more than pocket change!"

A troubled silence fell over the room. Jan, sensing his wife's gaze, finally forced himself to say something.

"Money isn't the problem. It's just not an easy thing to do at present . . ."

Another possibility then occurred to Anna.

"You mentioned a couple of times," she began, turning to face her husband, "that your typist has a lot of connections. Her name is Marta, right?

"Yes," Jan muttered.

"Why don't you talk to her?"

"She doesn't work for us anymore."

"Really?" Anna was surprised. "Why not? You always spoke so highly of her . . ."

"She quit . . ." he retorted, frowning. "She found some other occupation."

"What about your brother?" asked Irena.

Jan looked at his wife.

"Well, yes! But where is he now, anyway? I really do wonder just what has happened to him. Has he left town again?"

"It would appear so," Anna replied, blushing lightly.

However, he did not notice.

"What a pity!" Jan said. "And this is the one time he really could have been of some use to us. Although his contacts are probably nothing out of the ordinary. So he's out of the question. Who does that leave us with?"

Suddenly a thought occurred to him.

"What about Fela Ptaszycka? Have you seen her lately?" he asked Irena. "Whatever happened to her? I haven't seen her for such a long time."

"Me either."

"Maybe she could help us somehow. I remember it used to be that . . ."

"I doubt it," Irena cut him off.

"You don't think so? Not even for your sake?"

She shrugged.

"People change."

"Fela?" he was surprised. "Why would you say that? How has she changed?"

"In a fundamental way!" she said, smiling bitterly. "She has some ONR[8] guy hanging around her. She's head over heels in love with him. You figure out the rest."

"That's unbelievable! Our Fela?"

"Our Fela."

"What, she's become an anti-Semite? That's hard to imagine."

"But there you have it."

"Unbelievable," he repeated.

Irena mechanically leafed through several pages of the Breughel album.

"I haven't seen her in almost six months. Maybe she's gotten over it."

"Let's hope so," Jan pondered. "In any case, I'll go and see her. I'll at least try . . ."

"Do that," she replied indifferently.

|||

Toward the end of supper, which transpired in much the same atmosphere as on the previous evening, Władek stopped by at the Maleckis'. He was freshly washed and ruddy, not a hair out of place. Stepping into the hallway to meet him, Malecki immediately detected the scent of fine lavender water.

"The councillor would like to see you, sir," Władek said, bowing, "if you have a moment and would be good enough to stop by and see him."

"Fine," Malecki replied. "I'll be there in fifteen minutes or so."

"Thank you most kindly," Władek said, smiling politely. "The councillor will be waiting."

Malecki pensively returned to the living room.

"Zamojski wants to see me . . ." he said, sitting down at the table.

A moment later he pondered out loud.

"I wonder what sort of business he could have with me?"

As soon as supper was over, he rang at the apartment across the hall. The former councillor was sitting in his study. Still holding the book he had been reading, he emerged from behind his huge desk.

"Do come in, sir," he said, politely motioning Malecki to an armchair. "Pardon me for troubling you, but I'm a trifle unwell myself . . ."

He was wearing a dark smoking jacket and had house slippers on his feet. Indeed, he did not look well. Taking a seat opposite Malecki, he set the book aside on the table beside him.

"I'm brushing up on *Pan Tadeusz*," he explained. "It takes one's mind off things . . ."

Knowing the landlord's penchant for idle chatter, Malecki did not wish to allow him to get into any further personal revelations.

"How may I help you?" he said formally.

Zamojski was startled by this abruptness. He had prepared in advance a longish disquisition upon the beauties of Mickiewicz's poem, intending later to segue artfully into affairs of the present day and only then, in an atmosphere of confidentiality and intellectual understanding, to take up in their connection the sensitive matter that formed the basis of the interview. Now Malecki had thrown his all plans into disarray, and Zamojski found himself incapable of conducting the entire conversation.

Malecki guessed what Zamojski wanted and, for his part, did not intend to make it any easier for him. He felt a surge of anger toward Irena. He was certain she must have gone out onto the balcony again, casting caution to the winds. For a good while both men remained silent. Zamojski's nose seemed to grow longer with the passing moments. Finally the councillor gathered together his scattered thoughts.

"I wanted to speak with you, sir, about a certain matter . . ." he began. "Of course, this is totally confidential. The matter is possibly a bit drastic . . ."

He stopped, and with slightly reddened eyes he looked at Malecki for some kindly help.

"I am listening," Malecki said, disregarding Zamojski's courteous offer of an opening.

Zamojski sighed. He saw that he had to go it alone.

"If I am not mistaken, there is staying with you a certain Miss . . . I'm sorry . . . I do not know the lady's last name."

"Miss Grabowski," Malecki calmly explained. "We are putting her up for a few days. Is this about her tenant registration?"

"Yes and no," he said, cleverly avoiding the trap. "Of course, registration in its own good time, of course. But these days, you see, it's not so much registration I'm worried about . . ."

"I see," Malecki admitted agreeably.

"It's just that . . ."

"Just that what?"

"Pardon me for putting it this way," he said, collecting himself, "but certain facts have come to my attention . . ." He paused. "No, more than that, I am almost certain, yes, almost certain . . . " he repeated with emphasis, "that Miss Grabowski's heritage . . ." He paused again. "Excuse me for asking," he said, anticipating Malecki's answer, "but is that really the lady's last name?"

As he posed this question, which anxiety had forced out of him, his nose grew even longer and his reddened eyes darted wildly about, as if each of them wanted to bore itself into Malecki. For a moment Jan was silent. He was surprised not so much by the question itself, which he had expected, as by the councillor's appearance. At first he could not quite understand why Zamojski's face suddenly seemed so new to him. Then suddenly he was struck with a revelation: his face was Semitic. That face, betrayed at that moment by its eyes, was beyond any shadow of a doubt the face of a Jew. Impulsively he cast his gaze over the dark portraits solemnly peering down from the walls, and suddenly he did not feel like playing this game of deception any longer.

"Councillor," he said, leaning toward him in friendly fashion, "let us suppose that I answer your question in the negative. Let us say that Grabowski is not her real name. In that case, sir, what do you advise me to do?"

Zamojski sank in panic even more deeply into his armchair.

"I don't want to know anything about it!"

Malecki sensed he was gaining ground.

"Excuse me, sir, but you yourself said that our conversation was to be held in strictest confidence, so I am entitled to speak openly, am I not? And it is only for that reason that I am asking you what, in your opinion, do you think I should do?"

Zamojski stared at his guest dolefully. One could read in his expression a clear reproach for having been dragged into the dark affairs of others.

"Please forgive me," he finally blurted out, "but how should I know what to do? I'm as sorry as anyone about what is going on. But there are people living here, you have to understand. So many people . . . women, children . . . If something should happen, like an inspection or, God forbid, someone going to the police . . . You surely know what I mean?"

"Yes," Malecki freely admitted, "but what should I do?"

Zamojski, pressed for an answer now for the third time, could stand it no longer. The remnants of restraint abandoned him, and he gave in to his own distress. Grabbing himself by the head, he began to moan.

"Christ Almighty, why are you doing this? What is it you want from me? I have nightmares about the Gestapo as it is. It's enough to drive a person to the brink, for Christ's sake."

Malecki waited for him to calm down. After a decent pause he spoke in a sympathetic and entirely friendly tone.

"Please believe me, councillor, I understand everything perfectly well. But we are talking about a person's life here."

Zamojski shrank into himself and remained silent.

"I know, I know," he finally muttered, inclining his head. "One must respect human life . . ."

Malecki immediately went on the offensive again.

"I can assure you, sir, that Miss Grabowski will not stay here any longer than is necessary, no longer than a few days. You surely understand that because of my wife's condition it lies in my own interest as well. It is a matter of a few days at most. But if you will allow me one last indiscreet question, for I don't want there to be any misunderstandings, how was it that you learned that someone was staying in our apartment? Have you yourself seen Miss Grabowski?"

Zamojski denied it with the shake of his head.

"So someone informed you of it? May I ask who? Someone from this house?"

The councillor hesitated.

"Mrs. Piotrowski?" Malecki suggested.

The councillor confirmed it silently.

"Well, then, it will be necessary to calm her down," Malecki decided. "To explain to her that she was mistaken. To tell her that Miss Grabowski's appearance really does arouse suspicion, but that . . . and so on . . ."

Zamojski looked completely spent. He nodded in assent without saying a word. It ended with their agreeing that Malecki would personally have a conversation with Mrs. Piotrowski to put everything in the right light. He offered to do so himself, wanting to help Zamojski out. A moment later, to be sure, he regretted this hasty step, but he could not take it back. On the whole, everything had gone much better than expected. On parting, he wanted to express his indebtedness and gratitude to Zamojski.

"Not everyone in your place would have acted as you did!"

The councillor blushed like a little boy. He relaxed a little and, still flushed with embarrassment, said with unexpected force:

"With one reservation, sir! Every 'virtuous Pole,'" as the poet says, would have done exactly the same and not otherwise."

His small face, burdened by his too-large nose, at that moment seemed to Malecki almost like those on the old-fashioned portraits looming darkly in the depths of the room.

On his walk downstairs he lost the resolve to talk to Mrs. Piotrowski and decided to put it off until the following day.

Chapter 5 ılı

GOOD FRIDAY ARRIVED, the fifth day of the insurgents' resistance. Fires burrowed ever more deeply into the heart of the ghetto. Amid the smoke and blaze, ceaseless gunfire resounded, and the dry rattle of machine-gun and automatic rifle fire rang out without pause.

The Germans also began to hunt down Jews in the city proper. At various times and places individual Jews had managed to escape beyond the walls, and now reinforced German and Ukrainian patrols, joined by detachments of navy-blue police,[1] were tracking down escapees on the streets of town. Guardhouses were set up near manhole covers, since that was the most frequent route Jews used to reach freedom. Those caught were executed on the spot. Throughout the day in various parts of Warsaw, short bursts of rifle fire could be heard. The sound would cause panic on the streets, sending pedestrians scurrying into doorways for cover. Every so often a solitary hunched-over man would come running across a suddenly deserted square or street, only to be cut down by a salvo of machine-gun fire and fall flat on the pavement. Ukrainian policemen in their green uniforms would come riding up on bicycles and finish off any still alive. In a moment, traffic on the street would return to normal.

Throngs of people crowded in front of the churches on their way to Good Friday services. It was the most beautiful spring day imaginable.

Malecki did not go to see Mrs. Piotrowski that morning. Availing himself of the likelihood of her being out at that time of day, he put off the unpleasant conversation until later that afternoon. Instead, he decided to pay a visit to Fela Ptaszycka.

Fela lived in a villa belonging to her mother, a despotic old woman entirely under the domination of her own selfishness, the widow of a Polish landowner from Ukraine. Malecki recalled from former times, when he had seen a lot of Fela, that the painter had often complained about her unpleasant living situation. Still, she loved her quarrelsome mother and because of her could never quite make up her mind to move out.

The villa stood back from the boulevard along the Vistula, somewhat isolated, separated by an empty lot from a row of other nearby houses. It was surrounded by a small but thickly planted old garden engulfed in burdocks. It was not without some feeling that Malecki pushed the buzzer at the entry, for he had not seen Fela in more than a year. Having known her well from before, he could not accept that everything Irena had said about her would prove to be true. He waited quite some time for someone to answer the door.

The sun in full glory filled the high, bright stairwell. One could smell lilacs blooming, and the clean, fresh air was full of the merry twitter of birds. On the other side of the boulevard flowed the Vistula, bathed in sunlight as if entirely covered with sparkling, liquid gold. Behind it rose Warsaw with its bluish cloud of fog-shrouded houses and its gleam of slender church towers. Over the city, heavy and immobile, hung a black cloud of smoke from the fires. A small red kayak floated down the middle of the river.

Malecki rang once again, and in another moment he heard steps approaching. When Fela opened the door, it seemed to Malecki that she did not recognize him at first.

"Hello, Fela!" he said, moving into the shadow to hide from the sun. "Don't you recognize your old friend?"

At first she seemed caught off guard, but then she responded immediately with her plain, boisterous cordiality, as abundant as her massive body.

With an energetic, almost masculine movement, she pulled him into the hallway.

"So you finally remembered me!" she declared.

She still seemed confused, however, and most evidently surprised by his unexpected visit.

"Am I interrupting something?" he asked.

"No, no, of course not!" she answered hurriedly. "If you can just wait a second, all right?"

She looked around the hall for a place to put her guest.

"Oh, come on in here!" she said, opening the door to a small living room. "Make yourself comfortable. I'll be back in a minute. I have just one thing to take care of upstairs. It won't take long . . ."

"Don't hurry for my sake," he said, laughing. "I can wait."

Only now that he could see Fela in full light, did he perceive how much she had changed since he had last seen her. In the course of those months she had aged several years. The hair at her temples was gray. The features of her too-large face, though carefully toned with lipstick and rouge, seemed even more irregular than before. Her physique reminded one of a brawny giantess, but her face looked like that of an ugly and prematurely aging woman. And she was not even forty.

"So wait here for me here, all right?" she repeated.

From the doorway she looked back at him warmly.

"I'm very glad you've come," she said in her stentorian voice, unsuccessfully trying to lend it a trace of intimacy. "You can't even imagine what an important day this is for me . . ."

Malecki hesitated.

"Do you know who is staying with us?" he finally decided to say. "Irena Lilien."

"Irena?" Fela said joyfully. "You don't say! So she's still alive?"

"Yes."

Fela fell to thinking.

"I've thought so much about her lately. I have such a guilty conscience on her account. But I have to go," she said, remembering about her business. "We'll talk about it later. Bye-bye for now!"

Malecki had been prepared to wait for several minutes at most, but after fifteen minutes Fela had still not returned. In his impatience he began to pace back and forth across the cramped living room, cluttered with furniture. Fela's brief business, it appeared, was turning into a long and dragged-out conversation. Several times he hesitated at the door and tried to listen for the sound of voices from upstairs, but there was nothing but silence. The house gave the impression of being deserted.

Tired of knocking against the furniture, he went to the window and looked out on the small garden and, beyond it, the Vistula. At that very moment a large green automobile drove past on the street outside, bearing stiff-backed German policemen wearing helmets and carrying automatic rifles. A small gray bird was twittering and hopping gaily about in a sun-drenched lilac bush. Now the boulevard was completely empty, but soon there came a boy and girl walking hand in hand. Both were fair-haired and dressed in springtime clothing, he in linen pants and a blue shirt, she in a light yellow dress.

Malecki leaned against the windowsill, squinting and taking in the broad landscape of Warsaw and the Vistula. At that moment the dull thud of two shots, like handclaps, could be heard from the floor above. Malecki started, but did not move, paralyzed by his initial reaction of utter terror. He held his breath and listened, but he could hear no sound from the interior of the house. It was utterly silent and so peaceful that for a moment it seemed to him either that he must have misheard or that the two shots had come from the street outside. Calming down somewhat, but with his heart still racing, he approached the door, opened it, and peered into the hall.

Suddenly a door slammed shut upstairs and the hurried footsteps of at least two men could be heard running down the stairs. Before he could make it back into the living room, the two of them appeared on the landing and instantly spotted him. Startled, they hesitated only for a moment and then simultaneously made the same unmistakable motion of reaching for a weapon hidden in their coats.

Both were young and dressed in civilian clothing, wearing jackets and tall boots. At first Malecki took them for German agents, and it was only when they descended into the hall that he recognized one of them—a tall blond with penetrating, deep-set eyes—as the Zalewski who had been paying visits to the firm. He immediately connected his presence here with Irena's account the previous day about Fela's recent affairs. "They've killed her!" the thought quickly glanced off the surface of his consciousness, and a penetrating chill gripped him.

Zalewski also recognized him, and a dark flush came over his face and brow.

"What are you doing here?"

Malecki looked from one to the other. He only now noticed that the other man, a broad-shouldered, brown-haired fellow who was standing gloomily nearby, held a revolver in his hand.

"What have you done with Fela?" he asked in a stifled voice.

The brown-haired man looked at Zalewski.

"Do you know him?" he nodded toward Malecki.

Zalewski nodded back silently in assent.

"What sort of guy is he? Does he know you, too?"

Zalewski, leaning toward his comrade, whispered several words in his ear. The brown-haired man bit his lip and glared at Malecki from under his brow.

"No, wait . . ." Zalewski said, starting toward Malecki.

Jan instinctively backed up against the wall. But as soon as his shoulders touched its surface, a short shot rang out. Malecki swayed, and his hand clutched his chest. He balanced on his toes and remained suspended there for a moment, as if holding a ballet pose. Suddenly, making a half-turn, he fell on his back. Zalewski, standing nearby, barely had time to step aside.

It became so quiet that through the open door of the little parlor one could hear the chirping of birds outside. The glare of the sun reached as far as the threshold of the hallway. There it broke off, but even the depths of the entryway were flooded by strips of brightness.

Rustling his wide jacket, the dark-haired man leaned over the body of the man lying on the floor and for a moment looked him over carefully. At last he waved his hand, straightened up, and turned toward his companion, who stood looking, very pale and with his head bowed.

"Well?" he said, nudging him on the shoulder.

Zalewski did not move. His companion stuffed his weapon back in his coat pocket.

"No need to dwell on things. Everything's quite clear. We had to get rid of him, or he could have given us away. And that would have been the end!"

He stepped quickly over the corpse lying in the doorway and, entering the parlor, approached the window. He looked for a moment out onto the street.

"All's clear!" he declared, returning to the hall. "We can leave."

Suddenly, he struck his forehead with the palm of his hand.

"We forgot the most important thing!"

He knelt down next to the corpse and, taking the wallet from its jacket pocket, began looking intently through the papers in it.

"What are you doing?" asked Zalewski.

"We still have to take his papers off him," the other retorted, taking out some documents. "Do we have to make things any easier for the police?"

He stuffed a few scraps of paper into his coat and restored the wallet to its place.

"All right!" he said, casting a glance at Zalewski. "Let's go, shall we?"

The man straightened up.

"Of course!"

"Thank God! I thought you were losing it."

Zalewski scowled disdainfully.

"Me? You must not know me very well. Let's go!"

The dark-haired man was already standing at the door.

"Listen, Zygmunt, you weren't in love with Fela, were you?"

"Are you crazy?" Zalewski shrugged. "With that old bag? We needed her, that was all."

"I know," the man readily agreed. "But she also knew too much about us!"

Zalewski bit his narrowed, pursed lips.

"The idiot!" he muttered. "Who did she think she was, anyway? Did she think we were just going to let her walk away?"

"Maybe she did! But in the end she wasn't the least bit frightened when she saw the gun . . ."

"You don't think so?" Zalewski considered.

"But that other guy was clearly scared stiff . . ."

"That's for sure!" Zalewski laughed. "What a coward! I had him pegged from the beginning. The mentality of a rotten intellectual."

"Oh, yeah?" the other asked, interestedly. "A liberal?"

"Something like that."

The brown-haired man clapped his comrade on the shoulder.

"So, you see, by odd coincidence we get to chalk up an additional good deed!"

Both burst out laughing, and they were still laughing merrily and carefree a moment later, when they were outside and walking at a brisk pace along the sun-drenched boulevard.

At that moment a tiny, gray-haired old woman approached them from the opposite direction, stepping gingerly and leaning on a thin cane. She wore a yellowed lace collar at her neck, an old-fashioned dark-green velvet coat, and black mittens on her stiff, arthritic hands. She looked at them curiously with her faded, once-blue eyes. As they passed, she stopped and turned around. Stooped over and leaning on her cane, taking in the springtime sun, she watched with a good-natured smile as the boys walked away.

|||

Until noon Anna's day had passed peacefully. In the course of her everyday household chores she had conversed at length with Irena, and together they decided it would be best for her to head for the countryside upon receiving her new documents. Jan still had lots of contacts from prewar times among landowning circles, so now seemed like a good time to make use of them and try to arrange for a stay on some reasonably safe estate. If such a solution were to run into problems or for one reason or another to become impossible, there was still another solution: to place Irena in Grotnica, the old Cistercian cloister Jan had once begun restoring. This plan appealed to Irena most of all. She was not aware of the current situation there, nor could Anna tell her much about it, but both imagined that Grotnica, located far from the railroad line and situated in a beautiful region at the foot of the mountains, would provide, behind the walls of a medieval monastery, an ideal haven. The obstacles involved in getting to this far-off and unknown place seemed to them slight and easily surmounted. Both of them, although each for different reasons—Anna out of the goodness of her heart, and Irena out of helplessness and exhaustion—placed their hopes in their ability to avert bad fortune. Only when Anna touched on the end of the war and the new life that everybody would get to start over, did Irena become silent and lost in thought. but the next moment she brightened up, and they talked about Grotnica in even greater detail. Anna was certain that Jan would like this plan as well.

It was not until around two o'clock that she began to worry that Jan had not returned, for he had promised to come back for dinner no later than one o'clock. When the clock struck three, and then four, she calmed down a bit. She thought that he must have had to take care of some unforeseen business and, for that reason, would not be returning before evening.

Since she did not want to neglect Good Friday traditions, she decided to leave the house for a while and drop in on the Tomb service[2] at the nearby church in Wawrzyszew. The hour was not late, barely after five, so she could count on making it back home before Jan returned.

On the stairs she ran into Tereska Karski. Wearing a fresh pink dress and carrying her beloved doll in her arms, she was hopping up and down the steps singing to herself.

Anna stroked the girl's dark, silken hair.

"Where's mamusia, Tereska?"

"She's gone to town," she replied, intoning her "la-la-la" and hopping down a step.

"Be careful not to fall, Tereska," Anna warned her. "You could hurt yourself." Tereska's "la-la-la" followed her down the stairs.

The afternoon was warm and beautiful, practically summerlike. A cloud of smoke still hung over Warsaw, and, since the wind was blowing from that direction, out of the south, here too the air was saturated with heat and wore a hazy tint.

Just then, people were heading her way from the streetcar stop, so she stopped a moment by the gate of her house to make sure Jan was not among them. For the most part the people returning from town were workers from Wawrzyszew. Dusty and tired, they passed by quickly, one after the other, almost every one of them carrying a package under his arm and some of them with a bottle of vodka protruding from their jacket pocket. At the tail end teetered the frail and emaciated remnant of a man wearing a sports coat too big for him and long, baggy trousers gathered around him like an accordion. He walked with his head down, waving his arms and muttering something to himself. A scrawny, beak-nosed, thin-lipped woman, just as disreputable-looking as he, kept trying to block his way, now from one side and then from the other, threatening him with clenched fists and yammering at him incessantly. The drunken man kept trying to shake her off like a horsefly. They finally disappeared behind the corner of the house. Jan did not appear.

At a short distance from the house, she encountered the Piotrowskis along with Wacek and the young Osipowicz, evidently returning from the church service in Wawrzyszew. Both Piotrowskis were decked out in holiday garb, he in a light-colored suit, smart brown shoes, and a hat tilted jauntily over his low brow, and she in a very tight green silk dress, also wearing a hat and carrying a parasol with which she carefully shaded her sunburnt face from the sun.

Wacek and Stefanek lingered far to the rear, since their constant squatting down and their digging of pits in the sand took a lot of time. Wacek performed the work much more quickly than his comrade. When a pit was ready—and they were ready in the wink of an eye—he would hop into it and sit down. Then, twisting his head about, he would imitate the cackling of a hen laying an egg. Little Osipowicz emulated his comrade assiduously, but he could not manage to cackle. He turned red as a beet, and his small, faded eyes clouded over from the effort, but all he could get out of his distended little throat was a pathetic chirp.

Passing by Anna, Piotrowski examined her with the appraising eyes of a typical Warsaw rake.

"Have a pleasant walk!" he said merrily, lightly tipping the brim of his panama hat.

Mrs. Piotrowski stiffly straightened her back and began looking for her son.

"Wacek!" she cried in an unnatural voice, twisting her lips.

Just beyond the last houses in the Bielany development, the village of Wawrzyszew began. First one had to wade across a fairly broad area of sand whose dry and wavy expanse marked where a spruce forest, cut down in the course of the war, had once stood. Somewhat farther along stretched a meadow, yellow with cowslip blossoms. Silvery strips of young rye, just sprouted but quite abundant given the early time of year, undulated lazily in the breeze. Goats grazed in the meadow, and among them gamboled a fair number of snowy-white kids.

The shortest road to the Wawrzyszew church bypassed the village. The suburban workers' settlement, with its small brick houses, was off to one side, while a path wound between tall and as yet leafless linden trees, skirted the edge of some small, shallow ponds, and then led across a field between pastureland and rye fields. The meadows bloomed with the ubiquitous golden cowslip, as yellow as the air was clear and the heavens blue. Blackthorn bloomed on the steep bank of one of the ponds. Like fluffy, motionless clouds, they cast their sharp reflections in the greenish water.

Anna, a little fatigued, sat down for a moment on the edge of the slope. A thicket of blackthorn was right beneath her, and, as she stretched out her hand, she could easily touch the delicate blossoms. Some had already fallen off, and the green slope was lightly strewn with white flakes.

The explosions in town reached even here, and the smoke from the fire seemed larger and gloomier than from in front of the house. The entire town was drowning in an immense, black cloud.

Next to the water and the springtime fields, however, it was so peaceful and quiet that she wanted to take advantage of this brief moment of solitude and try to take in the last few days, to think things over, and to set them straight in her mind.

She had never learned to live life in a rush and was never able to feel right toward herself or those nearest to her until she had managed to absorb into the fullness of her being the overflow of feelings and experiences with which she was inevitably assailed. Nothing tired her more than the sporadic, chaotic, and ever-changing nature of things. It was in her nature to give everything a name and to assign a value to it. But she had barely begun to think about the week that had passed when she realized that there were so many fresh impressions that she was unable to assimilate them all. She soon stood up and continued walking.

The little church in Wawrzyszew stood off by itself in a field, amid old linden trees and slender Vistula poplars. Since the first green buds had barely had time to appear on the trees, the church's white baroque facade was sharply outlined against their brown trunks and blue-gray branches. It was a typical village church, old and secluded. Nearby, on a treeless hill, numerous crosses and graves came right up to the road, since the Germans had taken down the cemetery's iron fence during the war. For that reason, the small cemetery wore a sad expression of emptiness and neglect. High above it rose a solitary wooden cross marking the mass grave of soldiers fallen in defense of Warsaw in September 1939.[3]

Anna paid a visit to the cemetery before entering the church. The soldiers' graves, almost all of them without inscriptions and marked only by small birch crosses, were arranged in straight, even rows, all identical, small, and overgrown with a blanket of springtime green. The graves were very many. Some were bedecked with flowers: village bouquets of marigolds, and here and there branches of lilac and blackthorn. Beneath the tall cross rested a rusty soldier's helmet, above which two Polish banners were crossed, the paper already a bit tattered and faded. It was very quiet. A diminutive old lady in a headscarf and a fair-haired young girl were cleaning the narrow, sandy paths between the graves. Not a single tree grew here, all of them having been cut down by locals during the difficult winters of the war.

Besides the old woman and young girl tidying up, there was no one else around. The sun, already setting in the west, still warmed with its rays, and a late afternoon calm had settled on the place. Crickets rustled nearby in the newly sprouting grass. Anna knelt at the foot of the cross and silently, almost automatically began to pray. After a moment, she realized she was praying for Julek. She buried her face in her hands and knelt for a long time without moving, her shoulders hunched. All at once she paled slightly and began to shake. The baby she carried was moving, more forcefully than it ever had before. Her heart began to pound. The child's motions were so strong that she could feel inside her the individual movements of tiny, unseen arms and legs. An unimaginable bliss welled up inside her at this inner tremor, but at the same time anxiety penetrated this communion with her own body. How could it be that in the midst of all this human suffering, death, and injustice, in such an unhappy and desperate world, she carried within her, in defiance of the annihilation taking place all around, this new creation, this hope of future joy? Among the thousands of women who were also to become mothers, she felt that she alone had been bestowed with this gift undeservedly. She shuddered at her own happiness. In a panic and conflict of feelings, she began to pray for a merciful fate.

The small church was full of people. A mild, sunlit glow radiated within its white walls. Inside it smelled strongly of greenery and incense. Two plump baroque angels in richly gilded raiment leaned out from behind the altar, holding their arms out in a pathetic pose. In the very center of the nave, a plaster figure of Christ reclined against the background of an oil-print decoration depicting the interior of a cave. Little girls in white dresses knelt all around. A large number of other little girls and boys who had stopped by the church only for a moment stood stiffly and awkwardly in the foyer, dressed in their holiday attire, silently staring at the Tomb. The nave was filled with kneeling women and old men. Several beggars from the neighborhood—old men and wrinkled, hunch-backed, ancient women—were sitting in the pews. All were singing the Bitter Laments.[4] Their simple, untrained voices—the wooden voices of the men, the shrill and droning voices of the women—were badly out of key, but the song's monotonous melody made up somewhat for the worst of the dissonance. At the end of each stanza the singing subsided, and from outside came the chirping of birds, as well as the boom of distant explosions.

|||

Mrs. Piotrowski, having arrived at home, sat down heavily in an armchair just as she was, in her hat and still clasping her pink parasol.

"Uff!" she groaned. "Damn, what horrible heat . . ."

Her shoes, recently purchased and worn today for the first time, had turned out to be too small, and the heels a little too high. She gave a sigh of relief as she took them off her swollen feet.

"Uff!" she groaned again and began to rub her aching feet and toes.

Mr. Piotrowski, meanwhile, had wandered off somewhere unobserved. He soon betrayed his whereabouts by the characteristic sound of his hand knocking against a bottle. She instantly guessed that he was in the kitchen looking for the cherry vodka she had set aside for the holiday.

"Józek!" she called out. "Shame on you! It's Good Friday!"[5]

He did not bother to reply. All was quiet in the kitchen. "He's drinking, the rascal!" she thought to herself bitterly. A moment later he poked his head into the main room, and she cast on him an appraising glance.

"You smell of booze!"

He merely laughed and, standing in front of the mirror, carefully began to comb his dark, shiny, slicked-down hair.

Mrs. Piotrowski wiped her sweaty brow with her handkerchief, but did not take her eyes off her husband.

"Admit it, how much did you have to drink? Probably a whole half bottle?"

"Oh, come on!" he shrugged, adjusting his tie. "Just a tiny drop, only enough to wet my whistle."

"Yeah, sure! I know you only too well! Lord Almighty, what a wretch I've married!"

He turned around and, smiling impudently, put his hands on his hips.

"What? Your husband doesn't suit you? You think you've done so badly?"

He seemed to her at that moment so attractive that a knot formed in her stomach.

"Really!" she muttered reluctantly. "What is it that I see in you, anyway!"

He laughed protractedly and looked about for his hat, which was lying on the bed. He picked it up and, carelessly placing it on his head, looked at himself again in the mirror.

"Just where do you think you're going?" she asked nervously.

"To a friend's," he answered evasively. "I've got some business to take care of."

Whistling, he walked out the door.

She fell to thinking for a moment about her bitter fate. When soon afterward, limping and panting from the heat, she went to the window dressed in nothing but her stockings in order to see which way her husband had gone, he was nowhere to be seen. "The rascal!" she thought angrily and regretfully. She could not figure out how he had managed to disappear so quickly.

Piotrowski had not left the house at all. Stealing a glance out the front door to see whether the coast was clear, he quickly turned back and walked up the stairs. On the landing he ran into Tereska. She was sitting on a rather low windowsill, wagging her finger and sternly remonstrating with her doll, stiffly laid out beside her.

Piotrowski stopped.

"Hey, little girl," he said, "Do you happen to know whether Mr. Malecki is at home? You didn't notice whether he has come back, did you?"

She looked at him with eyes full of surprise and shrugged her shoulders. Piotrowski hesitated for a moment. Then he felt the effects of the vodka begin to kick in and he whistled through his teeth. The next moment he was ringing the Maleckis' doorbell.

When she heard the bell, Irena was sure it was Jan. She put down her book and rose from the daybed. So certain was she that it was Jan, that she practically leaped backward in fright when she saw Piotrowski standing in the open door.

He did not enter, however.

"Is Mr. Malecki home?" he asked.

In her surprise she could think of nothing to say but no, at which Piotrowski smiled broadly, showing his strong, white teeth. Before she was able to recover, he had slipped inside with a nimble, almost catlike movement. He closed the door quietly behind him and turned the key in the lock.

"So at last we are alone!" he said, turning toward her, pushing his hat back from his brow, and standing with arms akimbo. During this brief moment Irena managed to gain control over her initial fright.

"What is the meaning of this?" she asked haughtily.

Piotrowski narrowed his eyes.

"Easy does it, easy does it," he drawled. "We have plenty of time. Can't you invite a guest inside?"

"What guest?" she responded scornfully.

Piotrowski moved closer. His eyes glistened, and his swarthy face darkened.

"I've wanted to meet you now for several days," he said in a quiet, thick voice. "Ever since I saw you on the balcony the other day. There just wasn't a chance until now."

He shoved his hands deep into his pockets and took her in with a burning, somewhat sidelong gaze.

"Well, so now, you see, an occasion has presented itself!" He again gave a toothy smile.

He stood so close that she could feel the heat of his alcohol-soaked breath on her face. She still did not step back.

"I don't understand what you're talking about," she said coldly. "What occasion are you talking about? What is the meaning of this?"

"You don't know?" he smiled impertinently.

"What is it you want?" she repeated. "Who are you, anyway?"

Suddenly she lost control.

"Get out of here this instant! Do you hear me?" she raised her voice, seeing he was not moving. "Do I have to call the superintendent?"

Piotrowski backed off.

"Please do!" he drawled. "Go ahead, the road is clear! Don't let me stop you . . ."

He hitched up his pants and, taking off his hat, hung it on a hook.

"Please, go ahead and call him. I'm not stopping you . . . Go right ahead."

She remained silent, while Piotrowski looked at her intently.

"What, you're not going to call him?" he said with a flash of his teeth. "In that case maybe you'd like to invite me inside."

She hesitated a moment, but quickly turned around and, straightening her hair with a quick motion, walked back into the room. She took a cigarette from a pack lying on the table, lit it, took a puff, and glanced back at Piotrowski, who was leaning in the doorway.

"I'm afraid I have to disappoint you," she said, carelessly flicking the ash into a vase, "Because . . ."

"Because why?" he interrupted.

"Because I don't have any money," she finished her sentence and looked him in the eye. "Your predecessors, or how should I put it . . . your fellow tradesmen have already beaten you to it."

Piotrowski turned slightly red.

"What are you telling me that for?" he said, shrugging his shoulders. "You think I'm after money?"

He spoke with so much conviction that Irena became confused.

"So what is it you do want?" she asked uncertainly.

He gave a short laugh in response and moved closer. A chair separated him from Irena, and he pushed it aside.

"Such a looker like you has to ask that?" he said, casting another side-long glance at her.

Only now did she realize what it was that he wanted, and before she could manage to step back he had grabbed her by the arms and pulled her close to him. He evidently did not expect any resistance, for with a single shove she was able to free herself from her assailant's grip and knock him away. He staggered and most likely would have fallen had he not caught hold of the edge of the table. The blood rushed to his head. He stood for a moment bent over, leaning against the table with clenched fists, glowering at Irena through narrowed eyes. She, in the meantime, had retreated to the wall and immediately saw that she had put herself in a trap.

On one side her escape was cut off by the large daybed and on the other by a low-hanging bookshelf. Straight ahead was a draftsman's table and Piotrowski standing next to it. He reached her in a single bound. She defended herself vigorously, and for a while they struggled in silence. Finally he managed to turn her over onto the daybed and crush her beneath his body. She stifled a scream as she felt her strength waning and found herself less and less able to defend herself. He, for his part, skillfully gripped her with one arm in such a way as to pin both her hands. Raising his hips while continuing to crush her beneath his chest, he hurriedly and impatiently undid his belt with his free hand and began to lower his trousers. Through her dress she could feel his hot, naked body tense with desire. She shuddered. Now certain of success, with his knees tangled in his dropped trousers, he drew himself up and tried to take off her underwear. She tore herself away with her last remaining strength. Knocking him slightly off balance, she was able to slide quickly out from underneath him. She now found herself on the floor.

Seeing that the door to the balcony was half open, she leaped toward it and, pushing it wide, hesitated in the doorway. From down below, behind the thick drapes, as if out of a fog, she heard children's voices. She was breathing heavily, and she automatically began to adjust her rolled-up skirt and wrinkled blouse.

Meanwhile, Piotrowski clumsily got up off the daybed, holding up his drooping pants with one hand. He staggered slightly and stood there for a moment with his shirttail comically hanging out from under his crumpled sports coat, stupefied and hazily casting his glassy, bloodshot eyes around the room. At last he hitched up his pants and, glaring at Irena standing motionless in the doorway, slowly began to put his clothing in order. Finally, he straightened up and smoothed his unruly hair with both hands. As soon as he made a move in her direction, Irena retreated beyond the doorway and out onto the balcony. The reddish reflection of the setting sun shone from the windows of the neighboring villas. The radiant air rippled with a grayish smoke very like to fine, diffuse ash.

Piotrowski did not try to come any closer, but stayed in the center of the room. He planted his hands in his pants pockets, an ugly grimace contorting his mouth. He stared at Irena like that for a while, and then, smiling mockingly, finally turned on his heels, and left the room.

In the hall he smoothed his hair once more and straightened his crooked tie. Then he donned his hat with the same malevolent smirk playing on his lips. For a moment he tried to listen to what Irena was doing, but no sound could be heard, so at last he took himself to the exit, turned the key, and, slamming the door behind him, began walking downstairs.

On the landing, Tereska Karski was kneeling on the edge of the windowsill, nearly half of her body leaning out over it. Piotrowski paid no attention to her and continued walking.

Suddenly he stopped dead in his tracks. Down below in the open door to his apartment stood his wife, massive and unmoving, her arms folded across her chest. Recovering from his initial reaction, he descended the last couple of steps.

"What are you sticking your head out here for?" he snarled.

She measured him with a contemptuous gaze, a burning hatred flickering in her small, piercing eyes.

"What have you been up to, you scum?"

She examined him carefully from top to bottom.

"I'm asking you, where have you been?"

"None of your damn business!" he snorted, trying to get past her into the apartment.

Still she blocked his way.

"None of my business, eh?" she lowered her voice threateningly.

At that moment the air was rent by the piercing shriek of a child.

||I

Irena did not return to the room. The few minutes it had taken Piotrowski to leave the apartment had seemed to her an eternity. She was not sure whether the man might have second thoughts and return. Only the sound of the door slamming set her mind at ease. She felt so faint that her legs began to give way, and she had to lean against the railing of the balcony to keep her balance.

Down below, in front of the entryway, young Piotrowski was lying on his back with his arms outstretched and his eyes closed. Stefanek Osipowicz was leaning over him with an air of concern.

"Why are you lying there like that? Better get up . . ."

"No!" Wacek replied decisively.

"But why?"

"Because I'm Jesus."

"You're Jesus?"

"And you're an angel. Bow down, because I'm hanging on the cross."

From the landing could be heard the thin voice of Tereska, as she leaned out of the window like a little pink cloud.

"What are you boys doing?"

"I'm Jesus!" Wacek hollered back from down below, opening one eye. "Come on down!"

Supporting herself with her tiny hands on the window molding, she leaned out so far that her dark mop of hair fell over her eyes. She was trying to brush it back when her other hand slipped off the molding. The little girl lost her balance, and the weight of her body pulled her down. She gave a short, sharp shriek.

Mrs. Piotrowski was the first to arrive on the scene. Seeing the girl lying on the ground, she clutched her head.

"Jesus Christ Almighty!" she cried out mightily. "What has happened? Oh, my dear Mother of God!"

Wacek, who had picked himself up off the ground, started hollering at the top of his lungs, while little Osipowicz, by contrast, looked on dumbstruck in terror.

"Tereska's killed herself, Tereska's killed herself!" Wacek wailed fearfully, stamping his feet and sticking his fingers in his ears.

At that moment Piotrowski poked his head outside and, seeing the girl lying motionless in the sand, tried to go over to have a closer look, but his wife shoved him away.

"Back off, you wretch!" she snarled. "A child is a sacred thing."

He shrugged and stepped aside.

In the meantime nearly all of the tenants, alarmed by Wacek's cries, had come running. First to arrive were the Osipowiczes, then Władek, and after a moment Zamojski himself appeared in his smoking jacket and slippers. People also began to appear in the windows of the neighboring villas. Two young boys—one with a scooter, the other with a wooden gun—came running from the street to the site of the accident and pushed themselves forward among the crowd.

"Look!" the boy with the scooter nudged his companion. "She's dead!"

The other boy merely nodded his head in consternation. The ten-year-old's childish eyes had an unhealthy gleam. Sticking out his tongue to see things better, he kept scratching his injured calf with his left hand.

"Get out of here!" Mrs. Piotrowski said to them, outraged. "You're all we need right now."

They jumped back slightly to one side. In the meantime, Władek and Mr. Osipowicz knelt down next to Tereska. They turned her on her back. Lying pale as a communion wafer, limp, and with eyes closed, she really did look dead.

"How is she?" Zamojski drew near.

Osipowicz pressed his ear to the little girl's chest and listened for a moment.

"She's alive! It seems that nothing has happened to her. She just lost consciousness."

"Someone should call for a doctor," Zamojski advised.

Mrs. Piotrowski forced her way between them.

"What? She's alive?"

Suddenly she saw Irena standing on the balcony leaning on the railing, and a rage flashed across her swollen face.

"It's that Jewish bitch!" she cried, raising her fist. "It's all her fault!"

All directed their gaze toward the balcony. Zamojski turned pale and bit his lip. A murmur of distress passed through the crowd. Only Piotrowski stood over to one side, smiling sardonically.

"Mrs. Piotrowski . . ." whispered Osipowicz.

"You Jewish bitch!" she roared at Irena hatefully.

Only now did Irena withdraw into the apartment, but her disappearance riled Mrs. Piotrowski all the more. Pushing aside the people standing nearest her and rustling in her tight silk dress, she ran like a fury into the entryway and reached the second floor in a flash.

"Open up!" she shouted, beating on the door with her fists. "Open up this instant!"

Irena stood for a moment in the middle of the room trembling, her hands clapped over her ears, all the blood drained from her face. Instinctively, she looked around for a place to hide. The pounding became more and more violent.

"Open up!" the woman barked hysterically.

Irena could stand the shouting no longer. Shaking and white-lipped, she ran into the hallway and opened the door.

Mrs. Piotrowski looked frightful. She was red-faced, disheveled, and foaming at the mouth.

"What is it you want?" Irena stammered.

"I'll show you what I want!" she screamed.

And seizing Irena by the hand, she pulled her down the stairs behind her. Only on the ground floor did Irena try to resist, but the woman violently shoved her out the door and into the crowd.

Irena looked about at the throng, barely conscious of what she was seeing. Osipowicz was holding Tereska in his arms. Everyone averted their eyes from Irena in embarrassment. And last she noticed Piotrowski standing over to one side with his hands in his pockets, leering at her derisively.

His wife took a deep breath. "Come on!" she waved her hand at Irena. "Away with you! Get out of here!"

The residents of the villa next door were beginning to gather on the other side of the wire-mesh fence.

"Look!" said the boy with the scooter, again nudging his comrade. "They've caught a Jew."

The other nodded, continuing the whole time to scratch his calf. Apart from that, no one said anything. Even Wacek stopped crying.

"Mrs. Piotrowski, how can you?" whispered Mrs. Osipowicz, all the while holding Stefanek, still dumb with fright, by the hand.

Mrs. Piotrowski turned toward her, standing with her hands on her hips.

"I'll show you how!" she retorted belligerently. "Does she deny she's a filthy Jew? Just let her try! Let her try! Go ahead, deny it!" she pressed Irena, who stood motionless. "See if you dare!"

It seemed to Irena that the woman wanted to strike her then and there.

"Please don't touch me!" she whispered.

Mrs. Piotrowski laughed contemptuously.

"And who would want to touch you?" She looked about and, feeling the authority of her hatred, shrieked imperiously: "Get out of here! Back to the ghetto with you! That's where kikes[6] like you belong! Get out, I say!"

"But Mrs. Piotrowski . . ." Mrs. Osipowicz whispered again.

But Mrs. Piotrowski was entirely under the power of her raging fury.

"Go on, do you understand?! Get the hell out of here!"

Just then, Tereska stirred in the arms of the scrawny Mr. Osipowicz and opened her eyes.

"Where's mamusia?" she whispered.

"She's coming," Osipowicz said bending down toward her, "she'll be here soon."

"And Włodek?" she asked.

"Him too."

Irena stood among these people who avoided looking at her and still did not move. Her heart, like a piece of living flesh, beat in her throat. Suddenly she felt a blind, violent hatred well up inside her. She straightened up.

"Fine! I'm leaving!" she said unnaturally loudly.

Now certain of her own superiority, she looked Mrs. Piotrowski straight in the face and said, "But may your little shit of a son break both his arms and legs!"

Mrs. Piotrowski paled and opened her mouth, completely taken aback. She gathered Wacek to herself and covered his face with her hands.

Irena looked at those surrounding her, at their confused and now suddenly frightened faces, and felt inside herself a burning hostile joy. She no longer thought about what she was saying.

"And may the rest of you all die like dogs!" escaped her vengeful lips. "May you all burn just like us! May they shoot each and every one of you! I hope they murder you all!"

She quickly turned around and, in the deathly silence that ensued, she started to walk slowly toward the gate. She opened the gate, crossed the street at a diagonal, and walked further along the sidewalk with calm, even, steady steps. As soon as she had turned into a side street, where nobody from the house could see her, she quickened her pace and then began to run.

Soon she found herself next to the streetcars and jumped into one of the departing cars. It was practically empty, because hardly anyone was going to the city at that late hour, especially on Good Friday. In the distance a powerful explosion rocked the air, and from the midst of the dark cloud of smoke there arose over the ghetto a blood-red glow.

Andrzej Wajda's Film *Holy Week*

ANDRZEJ WAJDA'S 1995 FILM *Holy Week* has an unusual position in Wajda's total work for being an almost total box-office flop. Viewership in Poland during its run in cinemas was estimated at an astonishingly low eight thousand.[1] Among its few awards was a special commendation at the 46th Berlin International Film Festival, presented not so much for the film itself as in connection with a lifetime achievement award for its maker. It is one of the few works by Poland's Academy Award–winning director not to be currently available on VHS or DVD or distributed in larger format, either inside or outside Poland.[2]

Wajda had contemplated making this film since the early 1960s, possibly as a German-Polish coproduction, but for various reasons having to do with changing political currents, it was not possible to realize this project until the mid-1990s.[3] As Paul Coates remarks, Andrzejewski's *Holy Week,* for reasons of its length, language, and structure, seems virtually preordained for filmic adaptation, much more so than his multilayered full-length novel *Ashes and Diamonds,* whose movie version went far toward establishing Wajda's reputation in the West.[4]

Wajda enlisted a number of actors appearing on-screen for the first time, but the quality of the acting is high. The casting, period settings, and especially the photography are excellent. There are many trademark imaginistic Wajda touches. The plot unfolds suspensefully, leading to a rapid-fire sequence of events culminating in a dramatic, even if well-mined, literary archetype: the scapegoating and forcible expulsion from a group of one member for being different (here, Jewish). Everything augured a successful cinematic run. What, then, was this film's problem?

As we know, the plot centers on the dilemma of a recently married Pole, Jan Malecki (played by Wojciech Malajkat), who has thrust upon him, at the

Jan Malecki (Wojciech Malajkat). Photo courtesy of Andrzej Wajda

Irena Lilien (Beata Fudalej). Photo courtesy of Andrzej Wajda

Anna Malecka (Magdalena Warzecha). Photo courtesy of Andrzej Wajda

Julek Malecki (Jakub Przebindowski). Photo courtesy of Andrzej Wajda

Piotrowska (Barbara Dykiel). Photo courtesy of Andrzej Wajda

Piotrowski (Cezary Pazura). Photo courtesy of Andrzej Wajda

height of the final Nazi Jewish extermination campaign and the ensuing Warsaw Ghetto uprising during Holy Week 1943, the decision whether to shelter
a Jewish woman acquaintance of his, Irena Lilien (played by Beata Fudalej).
Personal considerations begin to color the decisions of Malecki, as he both
worries about the safety of his family (his wife Anna, played by Magdalena
Warzecha, is pregnant) and at the same time feels increasingly estranged from
the woman with whom he had once been close, whom he had even courted.
Irena, for her part, has been changed and embittered by the traumas of her
wartime experiences, to the point where Malecki barely recognizes in her the
person he once knew. Once her presence in the small apartment building becomes known to the bottom-dwelling tenant Mrs. Piotrowski (Barbara Dykiel)
and her lascivious husband (Cezary Pazura), Irena's expulsion is only a matter
of time.

In many ways *Holy Week* is a classic Wajda piece, situated during World
War II, when the fate of the nation, and that of many individuals, was hanging in the balance. Themes of patriotism, heroism, and martyrdom are cast
against a backdrop of often dubious characters, questionable decisions, moral
incertitudes, and interventions of a perverse and indifferent fate.[5]

Both Andrzejewski's novel and Wajda's film for the most part avoid the
pitfalls of melodrama to which treatments of such themes so easily succumb,
an outcome facilitated by the unlovable personalities of Andrzejewski's two
main characters: the scornful Irena Lilien and the cold and indecisive Jan Malecki. Irena's character has been criticized for being unrepresentative of the
Jewish ghetto victims and of Polish Jewry generally.[6] There is some truth,
however, to a German critic's observation that Irena finds herself caught in
the middle of a Christian morality play in which she is doomed to play the
role of Jewish scapegoat.[7] Under such an interpretation, Irena's personality or
representativity is irrelevant. The fact that the Liliens were fully assimilated
and not religiously observant, even if Semitic in appearance, underscores the
senselessness of the persecution to which Irena and her family are exposed. It
is made plain that her acerbic and uncharitable nature has been shaped more
by her wartime traumas than by her cultural heritage. She momentarily shows
a better side when rummaging through baby clothes with Anna.

A trademark of Wajda's adaptations of literary works is his ability to em-
bellish the action with imagery not contained in the literary prototype but
that remains faithful to and, at its best, gives greater depth to the author's

Riders of the Apocalypse. Photo courtesy of Andrzej Wajda

original conception. A number of examples of this technique can be found in *Holy Week*.

The action is punctuated by the appearance of four sinister, gas-masked German motorcycle and sidecar riders who appear as messengers of death at critical moments in the action, including Malecki's capture and murder by Gestapo agents. The "riders of the Apocalypse," as Wajda refers to them in the script, serve to reinforce the image of the German occupation as a force of nature against which no resistance is possible.

The overriding recurring symbol in the film is undoubtedly the somber gray ghetto walls, which cut off all view of the tragedy unfolding inside. While the walls obviously have an objective function in the story, in Wajda's film they also assume the symbolic weight of representing the divide between Pole and Jew, both over the centuries and in the present instance. Wajda alludes to this divide in the film's final intertitle, set against the walls, moving the words from their place early in the novel to the end by way of epitaph:

> [N]ie ma pomiędzy ludźmi większego i bezwzględniejszego przedziału jak pomiędzy szczęściem jednych i cierpieniem drugich. Wiele spraw wielkich i drobnych rozdziela ludzi, lecz żadna tak dotkliwie jak nierówność losu.

The ghetto walls. Photo courtesy of Andrzej Wajda

[[T]here is among people no dividing line greater or more absolute than that between the happiness of some and the suffering of others. Affairs great and small divide people, yet none so sharply as the inequality of fate.]

These words are absent from the version of the film provided to the author of this essay by the director, perhaps because they were, in the end, judged to be unequal to the task of encapsulating the meaning of the story. After all, Malecki and Irena in the end share the same fate, not different or unequal ones.[8]

Wajda alludes to the merry-go-round image from Czesław Miłosz's widely anthologized poem "Campo di Fiori," when Jan's younger brother Julek and his young charge Włodek attempt to get a better view of access routes into the ghetto by standing up and swinging as high as they can in their chairs.[9] In Andrzejewski's novel the carousel is still under construction, and the only role it plays is as a stage for a German machine-gun emplacement. In Miłosz's poem, the up-and-running carousel symbolizes the depraved indifference of the Warsaw populace to the tragedy unfolding behind the ghetto walls. The viewer familiar with Miłosz and Andrzejewski's on-again, off-again real-life relationship can find special meaning in Wajda's attempt to synthetically unite, as it were, these two quite different authors in the same image.

Julek and Władek on the carousel. Photo courtesy of Andrzej Wajda

The merry-go-round scene is visually effective, but controversial. It has been criticized as the director's attempt to purify and redeem Miłosz's infamous symbol by associating it with Julek and his patriotic band of adolescent freedom fighters. The inert carousel in Andrzejewski's novel, as contrasted with its mobility in Miłosz's poem, was criticized by Artur Sandauer, who saw in it an example of Andrzejewski's attempt to soften the depiction of Warsaw's inhabitants.[10] During Holy Week, however, this object would have been in precisely the state of partial assembly Andrzejewski describes; it was being set up in anticipation of summer, not only of the upcoming Easter holiday. The ghetto uprising continued through the middle of May, by which time it would have been fully assembled and operational, as in Miłosz's poem. Since the action of *Holy Week* takes place against a backdrop of purported history, Wajda's transformed image verges on tampering with historical reality, as indeed Andrzejewski himself does with the entire subplot of Julek and his gang, for which there is scant justification.[11]

Wajda's film consciously plays up the connection between Julek's mentality and that of the later and equally ill-fated Warsaw insurgents, whom the Communists sometimes portrayed as unrealistic national romantics. In addi-

The hanging laundry scene, Anna and Julek. Photo courtesy of Andrzej Wajda

tion to casting Julek (played by Jakub Przebindowski) as the virtual double of Zbigniew Cybulski's Maciek in *Ashes and Diamonds* and thereby referencing his earlier and more popular film, Wajda recalls that movie's famous hanging laundry scene, when Julek comes to pay farewell to Anna before his suicide mission to bring help to the ghetto fighters. Whereas the bed linen in *Ashes and Diamonds* becomes stained with the hero's blood, here the wash is besmirched with last year's dead leaves, symbolizing the numberless Polish war dead, tossed up by an angry gust of wind coming as if out of nowhere. The crucifix in the Good Friday church service, dislodged and lying supine to represent the entombed Christ, calls to mind the upside-down crucifix hanging from the shattered rood screen in the bombed-out church in *Ashes and Diamonds.*

A major motivation in Andrzejewski's novel was to depict varieties of Polish anti-Semitism—a prickly topic in Poland, needless to say. Wajda goes to considerable lengths to tone down this aspect of the novel, not necessarily to the movie's benefit and in any case without winning it any more friends for his efforts. In the film's final cut, almost all overt expression of anti-Semitism

The Polish fascist Zalewski (Artur Barciś). Photo courtesy of Andrzej Wajda

has been limited to two shady characters, the black marketeer Mrs. Pio-trowski and the fascist agitator Zalewski (Artur Barciś). Mrs. Piotrowski's words undergo radical amelioration. In the novel her usual way of referring to Irena is *Żydowica,* which could be translated as "Jew-bitch." In the film this word does not occur, replaced by the relatively neutral *Żydówka,* "Jew-ess, Jewish woman." The extremely offensive slur *Srul,* associating the Yid-dish first name *Srulek* "Israel" and the Polish word *srać* "to shit," is expunged from Mrs. Piotrowski's final diatribe against Irena.

Irena's indifference to the suffering of the Poles is muted through the cut-ting (for the scene was contemplated in the original script) of a basement scene in which the ungrateful Irena is given water and a place to rest by a wretched Polish family displaced from the Poznań district, whose shell of a son has just been released from Auschwitz. Paul Coates suggests that this scene was cut due to the sensitivity of the modern viewer to the name Auschwitz which, since the novel was written, has acquired synonymity with the Nazi extermi-nation of the Jews.[12] At first the camp housed Russian and Polish prisoners; in spring 1943, when the novel was begun, the crematoria were just being built.

Wajda obviously does not need to give a history lesson here, but if the name "Auschwitz" were a concern, it could easily have been omitted without damage to the scene. The effect of this editorial decision is to lessen the number of instances in the film in which the Poles are seen to be suffering from the war as well as those in which Irena is shown in an unsympathetic light.

A scene from the novel showing the average Warsaw resident's indifference toward the Jewish plight, as spectators from the street comment derisively on a Jewish corpse dangling out of an apartment house's upper window, was contained in the shooting script but did not make the movie's final cut. Another vignette, part of the original film release but absent from the video provided to the present author by the director, depicts an occurrence from Malecki's travels to Mokotów to retrieve Irena's things from the Makowski family, with whom she had been staying. Along the way he witnesses a band of Polish urchins shrieking "Jew, Jew," while chasing across some potato fields an emaciated Jewish boy whom they have flushed out of hiding. The boy runs out into the street to be summarily executed by a passing German soldier. The effect of these editorial decisions is both to weaken the depiction of the broader context of the Warsaw wartime experience and to shorten the film almost to the point that it loses feature-length status.

The most radical adaptational liberty taken with the novel is also the most problematic, and it arguably lessens the effect of the film's concluding scenes. In the novel, Malecki, having found out that the Makowski family has been arrested for harboring Irena, decides to seek help from his and Irena's mutual friend from before the war, the sculptress Fela Ptaszycka, a colorful character entirely missing from the film. In so doing, Malecki inadvertently walks in on Fela's assassination by members of the ONR, an underground Polish fascist organization, and he himself is killed to keep him quiet.[13]

In the film version, Malecki is killed during his attempted visit to the Makowskis, of whose recent arrest Malecki is not then aware. As part of Wajda's seeming sanitization of the novel for easier domestic consumption, Malecki falls into a trap set not by fascist Poles but by German Gestapo agents (although this, too, is not made completely clear), who inexplicably choose not to capture him but to shoot him on the spot. The reason for the agents' shooting of Malecki is left unexplained. For all they know, he could have been an innocent visitor. If they thought otherwise, he would have been detained and interrogated, not shot, at least not at first. In the novel, Malecki's documents are taken from him by his murderers, and it is possible that he will not be identified. Even if he is, there is nothing incriminating about him that could lead back to his wife Anna or to Irena. In Wajda's film, however, Malecki is ostensibly shot on suspicion of harboring a Jew. He has his identification papers on him, and the tracks will certainly lead the Gestapo back to Anna, with tragic consequences, one can foresee, for Anna and her unborn child. In the novel, Anna's child is a symbol not of unending senseless tragedy but of redeeming hope for Poland after the war. By making Germans, not Poles, responsible for Malecki's death, Wajda, intentionally or not, introduces the distractive theme of "we Poles suffered too, and often because we tried to help you Jews," a motif that was muted in Andrzejewski's novel.

The motives and circumstances surrounding Malecki's death are not one of the strong points of the novel either. However, immediately afterward the reader of the novel becomes drawn into the rapid unfolding of Irena's story back in the suburb of Bielany. First, Mr. Piotrowski attempts to rape Irena, and then, in the next and culminating scene, the bigoted Mrs. Piotrowski falsely accuses Irena of causing an accident to one of the children in the house. Angry and envious of Irena for the effect she has on her husband, Mrs. Piotrowski yanks Irena from the Maleckis' apartment and forcibly expels her from the house to the accompaniment of a rain of abominable invective. An appalled but powerless crowd looks on, upon whom Irena casts her parting curse: *Dobrze, pójdę. A wy, żebyście wszyscy jak psy pozdychali! . . . żeby was wymordowano i wypalono tak, jak nas!* [Fine, I'll go. But as for you, may you all die like dogs! . . . May you all be murdered and incinerated just like us!]. After uttering this imprecation, toned down considerably from the novel, in which Mrs. Piotrowski's unpleasant son Wacek comes in for special treatment, Irena fatalistically boards a streetcar in the direction of the burning ghetto, to which she has been told by Mrs. Piotrowski "to return."

The shooting of Malecki is shown out of logical sequence in the film, coming after both the scene of the attempted rape and the scene of Irena's expulsion, diminishing the logical and dramatic crescendo of events that is so effective at the end of the novel. Malecki's shooting and Anna's synchronous praying in church are moved so that they follow Irena's banishment, incongruously inviting the interpretation that Malecki's death is a fulfillment of Irena's curse. To its enduring strength, the film ends with the haunting picture of Irena, impeccably dressed in her imported English blue linen

Irena's curse. Photo courtesy of Andrzej Wajda

suit, walking defiantly along the ghetto walls through a smoky haze, past a detachment of leering German soldiers, to an unknown but (given the symbolism of the smoke) assuredly tragic fate.

Catherine Axelrad suggests that at this end point Irena has recognized her identity as a Jew and desires to die alongside those in the ghetto, having accepted that as her destiny.[14] If so, the final scene of the movie constitutes a closing parenthesis with the film's initial scene—moved by Wajda from its more central place in the novel—in which Irena's father, sick and exhausted, commits a similar act by instinctively joining a long column of Jewish prisoners being escorted down a country road to their execution.

In her largely negative appraisal of the literary work on which the film is based, Madeline Levine singles out for special criticism the depiction of Irena's reversion to vengeful Old Testament stereotype at the end.[15] She also finds Anna Malecka's desire to help the Jews on the basis of Christian teaching condescending, for Anna is convinced that the Jews have erred by not accepting Christ. However, Anna's gentle and somewhat naive voice cannot be taken for that of the author. At the time the novel was written, Andrzejewski

Irena next to the ghetto walls (final scene). Photo courtesy of Andrzej Wajda

had broken with the Roman Catholic Church and was far from being its spokesman, much less an apologist for the role of the Church during the war. The innately good Anna leans on religion because it is both a part of her upbringing and a way of coping with a situation she is otherwise unable to encompass and internalize. It is not necessary to take her behavior as a comment on the superiority of Christian love to Irena's Old Testament desire for retribution. At this point in the action, it is impossible to understand Irena's actions as a commentary on much of anything. She is being hunted down like a dog, about to be driven to her death—it would be easy to comprehend her saying or doing any number of things. In the scapegoating scene there is a strong sense of Irena's conscious histrionic playing to the crowd by giving them what they both expect and fear: her curse and the evil Jewish eye, which is directed with special effectiveness at Mrs. Piotrowski's young son Wacek, whom his mother shields by placing her hands over his eyes. Irena defends herself with the only weapon at her disposal—the Jewishness imputed to her by the crowd—and it is not she who comes away from the scene looking the worse.

Councillor Zamojski (Wojciech Pszoniak). Photo courtesy of Andrzej Wajda

A far better locus for Andrzejewski's voice is to be found in the conflicted central character of Jan Malecki, whose conscience on behalf of his nation is rent by guilt over the fate of the Jews in a way religion cannot assuage, for he is not religious. It might be remembered that Jan had once courted Irena without giving any thought to her Jewishness. For all his vacillations and foibles, in the end, Malecki instinctively knows right from wrong. His viewpoint—and Andrzejewski's—is not that of Christianity but of a venerable Polish tradition of loyalty to friends and a humanistic tolerance of other peoples and faiths. In this tradition Malecki finds himself allied with the landlord Zamojski, himself of Jewish extraction, and his dictum that human life must be respected. The tradition of liberal tolerance is also reflected in Zamojski's escapist reading matter, a richly bound volume of Adam Mickiewicz's nineteenth-century verse novel, *Pan Tadeusz*, in which Pole and Jew are depicted as living peacefully and respectfully side by side.

Lacking in most commentary on *Holy Week* is an acknowledgment of the novel's scathing indictment of Roman Catholicism as practiced by the average Pole, including an implicit criticism of the Church as a source of moral guidance for the people during the war. Say what one will of Andrzejewski's motives, for he was at this date in the process of accommodating his writing to the requirements of the new Communist régime, this criticism is inherent to the title, structure, and conceptualization of the novel, in which the days of the Christian Holy Week are used to periodize and chronicle the final days of the Warsaw Ghetto.

In both novel and film religious substance is supplanted by holiday flutter, cant, gruesome symbols, and the ubiquitous use of empty religious exclamations. This picture is, needless to say, likely to be disturbing for a large number of Poles, who cannot but see themselves as vicariously indicted among the ice-cream eaters, carousel riders, Easter-loaf bakers, and hymn-singing churchgoers passing through the phases of Holy Week by rote, indifferent to the plight of the people on the other side of the ghetto wall, for whom the day marked the even more ancient holiday of Passover. Chillingly, Piotrowska's denunciation of Irena occurs on Good Friday, a day of special solemnity. The Good Friday service she has just attended seems to put her in an especially murderous frame of mind. The serving up of Irena as a sacrificial lamb at the same moment that Anna, in church, kisses the feet of Christ, is a deeply disturbing image not only for Catholic viewers; Catherine Axelrad, exaggeratedly, calls it "obscene."[16]

Two further scenes in the film come to mind in this general regard, both associated with Mrs. Piotrowski's obnoxious son Wacek. Since one episode appears early and the other late in the film, they serve to frame its central action in the same way that the film's initial and final scenes (the acceptance of their Jewish fate by Irena and her father) frame the work as a whole. As Malecki brings Irena home with him, he finds the children of the villa concentrated in the front yard under Wacek's command playing a game called "ghetto," consisting of enclosing a sandy terrain with a wall of refuse and shards of glass and then, presumably, bombing it. In the second scene, Wacek, just returned from the Good Friday service (Groby) at church, gives his own (mis)interpretation of what he has just witnessed by lying in the sand pretending to be Jesus "hanging on the cross." It is this childish game that induces the young girl Teresa, leaning out of an upper window while imagining herself to be an angel like the gilt ones at church, to lose her balance and tumble down into the yard.

Holy Week's "problem"—that is, why Wajda's film passed across the cinematographic landscape, as the director has said in a personal communication,

Wacek playing "ghetto." Photo courtesy of Andrzej Wajda

Wacek "hanging" on the Cross. Photo courtesy of Andrzej Wajda "without leaving a trace" (*przeszedł bez echa*)—has little to do with the film's artistic quality, which is fairly high. Like the novel, the film *Holy Week* makes Poles feel uncomfortable about their role in the Holocaust, which is depicted as largely passive and unsympathetic. Nor is the film pleasing to Jewish viewers who, without being able to raise objections about the verisimilitude of Irena's depiction, nevertheless would have preferred a more positive representative of their culture, and, no doubt, more attention paid to the Jewish insurgents who, in both the film and the novel, fight and die entirely off-screen.

A comparison of Wajda's film to the literary original and to the shooting script reveals a series of changes designed to make the film more palatable to the Polish audience toward which it was primarily directed. In so doing, Wajda, and possibly other editors, tampered with one of the signal characteristics of Andrzejewski's novel, its unflinching honesty of depiction, no matter how painful for his reading audience. While the director's changes do not go so far as to compromise the sense and integrity of the work on which the film is based, one would have much preferred a closer adaptation. There is probably no way Andrzejewski's work could be changed to make it politically correct enough to appeal to a general Polish viewership. This was a film that invited itself to be made but, at the same time, a film for which there was no natural audience, a contradiction that led to its inevitably disappointing performance at the box office.[17]

Notes

Notes on the Novel

Chapter 1

1. *Willa* (villa) generally refers to a large two- or three-story suburban residence, usually surrounded by a garden, either single-family or subdivided into a small number of apartments.

2. Fela Ptaszycka's last name recalls the word *ptaszek*, "birdie."

3. The Cistercian order, founded in 1098 near Dijon, France, is an offshoot of the Benedictines. The Cistercians were numerous in the lands of Austria-Hungary, including southeastern Poland.

4. Gestapo (from German Geheime Staatspolizei): the secret police of Nazi Germany, under the overall administration of the SS (see chapter 2, note 1, below).

5. Aryan papers: false identification papers indicating that the bearer is Polish, usually with a typical Polish last name such as "Nowak," "Kowalski," or, as in the Liliens' case, "Grabowski."

6. Saska Kępa (the Saxon Cluster), located on the east side of the Vistula directly south of the Poniatowski Bridge, was and is one of Warsaw's most desirable residential neighborhoods.

Chapter 2

1. SS (from German *Schutzstaffel*): security force, the paramilitary forces of the Nazi Party.

2. Germany invaded Poland on September 1, 1939.

3. Located in eastern Upper Silesia, approximately sixty kilometers west of Kraków, Auschwitz (Polish Oświęcim) at first incarcerated mainly Poles and, later, prisoners of all ethnicities and nationalities. As the war progressed, the camp became the extermination terminus for Jews transported from all over Europe. The first gas chambers and crematoria were installed in March 1943, about one month before the events described in the present novel.

4. Arconia: one of various student fraternal organizations popular at Polish universities during the 1930s, often taking part in the harassment of Jewish students. Arconia, to which Malecki belonged, was in fact one of the few such organizations to accept Jews as members. Arconians were a mythical race of superior beings. The fraternity survives to this day.

5. The Bug River formed the border between German-occupied Poland and Soviet-occupied Poland.

Chapter 3

1. *Charterhouse of Parma* (*La Chartreuse de Parme*): 1839 novel by Henri Stendhal, set in Napoleonic times.

2. About thirty kilometers north of Warsaw on the Vistula River, Modlin is the site of a historically significant fortress that played a major role in the defense of Warsaw at the outbreak of the war in September 1939.

3. Malecki is referring to the need to be off the streets by curfew.

4. The Zamoyskis were an ancient, enlightened, influential, and politically active Polish aristocratic family. Following old-fashioned spelling, the aristocratic name is commonly written with a *y* instead of a *j*. Andrzejewski attended the Jan Zamoyski *gimnazjum* (high school) in Warsaw, named after the sixteenth-century statesman and author, the founder of the Zamoyski Academy in the family seat in Zamość.

Chapter 4

1. August 6 Street. The date commemorates the creation of the clandestine National Government by Józef Piłsudski in 1914.

2. Because of a lack of gasoline, bicycle-powered rickshaws were a common means of transportation in Polish cities during the war.

3. Holy Week in Poland is accompanied by a thorough cleaning of the house, including the scrupulous washing of windows and the beating of rugs. The courtyards of Polish apartment houses often provide carpet-beating racks for the use of residents.

4. Hucul: an ethnic group from the Carpathian Mountains of western Ukraine, known for their handiwork and carpet designs of possibly Turkish influence.

5. Mrs. Piotrowski uses the word *Żydowica*, a highly derogatory expression utilizing the suffix *-ica*, commonly used to refer to the female of an animal species. The normal word for "Jewish woman, Jewess" is *Żydówka*.

6. *Pan Tadeusz:* celebrated novel in verse by the Polish Romantic poet Adam Mickiewicz (1798–1855).

7. Kercelak: an open-air bazaar (no longer existing) in the Wola district of Warsaw along Okopowa Street.

8. ONR (Obóz Narodowo-Radykalny, National-Radical Camp): an ultra-right-wing political group influenced by Nazism and with a profoundly anti-Semitic program, to which Zalewski belongs. The ONR was even more radical than the fascist-inspired Stronnictwo Narodowe (SN, National Party) founded by Roman Dmowski, of which it was an offshoot. Both groups were outlawed in Poland before the war.

9. Zamojski is referring here to the line from *Pan Tadeusz*, book XII, describing the Jewish tavern owner Jankiel: "Żyd poczciwy Ojczyznę jako Polak kochał!" (A virtuous Jew, he loved his fatherland as any Pole!).

Chapter 5

1. The Polish police collaborating with the Germans wore navy-blue uniforms, and were commonly referred to as the *policja granatowa*, or "navy-blue police."

2. The service, called Groby (tombs) in Polish, is described later. The corresponding service in English is the Veneration of the Cross.

3. A monument on this spot in the Wawrzyszew cemetery now reads, "Here rest 500 soldiers of the 30th Regiment of the Kanów Riflemen who perished valiantly in defense of their capital in September 1939. They were led by Major Bronisław Kamiński, who perished alongside them and was posthumously decorated with the Order of Virtuti Militari [Poland's highest award for bravery]."

4. Bitter Laments (Gorzkie żale): an ancient Polish chant sung at Easter time. Its contents retrace the Passion and Crucifixion of Christ, focusing on the sorrow of Mary.

5. Drinking alcohol on Good Friday, which is supposed to be devoted to somber religious contemplation, is an especially egregious offense in the eyes of the devout.

6. The word used by Piotrowska is *srul*, a particularly offensive Polish word of the time for Jews, based on the first name *Srulek*, or "Israel," and chosen because of similarity to the Polish word *srać*, "to shit."

Notes on the Afterword

An earlier version of this essay appeared in the *Polish Review* 50, no. 3 (2005): 343–53.

1. The statistic is from Marek Haltof, "Everything for Sale: Polish National Cinema after 1989," *Canadian Slavonic Papers* 39 (March–June 1997): 37. The film was shown on TV Polonia in early 2005.

2. The author is indebted to Andrzej Wajda for supplying him with a video copy of the film *Wielki Tydzień* and with an early version of the film's shooting script.

3. Interview with Wanda Wertenstein, "W realizacji—*Wielki Tydzień*," *Kino* 7–8 (1995): 29.

4. Paul Coates, "Observing the Observer: Andrzej Wajda's *Holy Week* (1995)," *Canadian Slavonic Papers* 42 (March–June 2000): 27.

5. In addition to Wajda's best-known wartime movie, *Ashes and Diamonds* (*Popiół i diament*, 1958), also based on an Andrzejewski novel, Wajda returns to World War II in *Kanal* (*Kanał*, 1957), *A Generation* (*Pokolenie*, 1955), *Lotna* (*Lotna*, 1959), *A Love in Germany* (*Eine Liebe in Deutschland*, 1983), *Dr. Korczak* (*Korczak*, 1990), and *The Ring with a Crowned Eagle* (*Pierścionek z orłem w koronie*, 1993).

6. See Madeline G. Levine, "The Ambiguity of Moral Outrage in Jerzy Andrzejewski's *Wielki Tydzień*," *Polish Review* 32, no. 4 (1987): 385–99. Levine's comments are, of course, directed at the novel, not the film, but Wajda's work is close enough to the novel in most respects, including its depiction of Irena, that one may selectively consider the published criticism of the novel as applicable to the film as well.

7. Gunter Göckenjan, "Jüdischer Humor," *Berliner Zeitung*, February 22, 1996, 18.

8. It is possible that the version of the film provided by the director was inadvertently the one abbreviated for television, in which case certain editorial decisions discussed here may not have been Wajda's but a studio editor's.

9. The carousel in question is of the old-fashioned type, consisting of twirling chairs suspended from long ropes in which one can stand and, by pulling on the ropes, swing further out and higher. The carousel in the film is set up right beneath the ghetto wall, so that on a particularly high swing one can see over it.

10. Artur Sandauer, *O sytuacji pisarza polskiego pochodzenia żydowskiego w XX wieku (Rzecz, którą nie ja powinienem był pisać)* [On the Situation of the Polish Writer of Jewish Heritage in the Twentieth Century (Something That I Myself Shouldn't Have Had to Write)] (Warsaw: Czytelnik, 1982), 38–39.

11. Reckoning that the time was not ripe for a general insurgency, the Polish underground provided the ghetto fighters with some small arms, rifles, hand grenades, and moral support, but with scant organized human assistance. Nevertheless, a small number of non-Jews were found among the ghetto dead, catalogued by German commander SS General Jürgen Stroop as "bandits," lending a certain credence to Julek's depiction.

12. Coates, "Observing the Observer," 28.

13. The letters ONR stand for Obóz Narodowo-Radykalny (National-Radical Camp). The party was outlawed in Poland before the war. The film scholar Paul Coates ("Observing the Observer," 30) misunderstands this scene both in the novel and in the film. Fela Ptaszycka is not, as Coates says, killed for being a Jew. In fact she is a Polish woman who has been flirting with the ONR but who now wants out

and so has to be killed. In the film, the murder scene has been completely transposed as to place, motive, and identity of the executioners. The fact that Coates does not catch this significant change is suggestive of the murky impressionism of Wajda's dramatization.

14. Catherine Axelrad, "La semaine sainte: Quelque chose d'obscène"(Holy Week: Something a Bit Obscene), *Positif* 423 (May 1996): 56.

15. Levine, "Ambiguity of Moral Outrage," 396–99.

16. Axelrad, "La semaine sainte," 57.

17. The author would like to thank his colleague Elżbieta Ostrowska for numerous perceptive and helpful observations both on Wajda's film and on this essay's original version.